# YOUR GHOST'S POSSESSION

## LACEY BUCKLES

This is a work of fiction. Names, characters, places, and incidents either are the product of the author's imagination or are used fictitiously. Any resemblance to actual persons, living or dead, events, or locales is entirely coincidental.

Copyright 2025 © Lacey Buckles

All rights reserved. No part of this book may be reproduced or used in any manner without written permission of the copyright owner except for the use of quotations in a book review.

ISBN 978-1-913673-23-9

*For the girl who chased shadows and listened for whispers, who believed haunted houses were just lonely places waiting for love.*

*And for Matt—thank you for seeing the heart in the darkness.*

# CONTENT WARNING

This story contains explicit sexual content, including MMF ménage dynamics, ghostly possession, and intense power exchange. Themes include obsession, loss, emotional manipulation, and blurred consent due to supernatural influence. The story also includes elements of horror, such as haunting, spectral violence, and past trauma.

This story contains:
- Explicit MMF ménage scenes
- Supernatural possession and influence
- Power exchange and emotional manipulation
- Blurred lines of consent (due to ghostly presence)
- Haunting and spectral violence
- Grief, obsession, and unresolved trauma
- Erotic horror elements, including ghostly sex

While all sexual interactions are ultimately consensual, some scenes explore dark, coercive, and unsettling dynamics. Please read with care and honour your boundaries.

# THE BOOKBINDER'S INVITATION

*This one is different.*

Not every desire is loud. Not every hunger bares its teeth.

Some haunt quietly—through touch that never lands, through whispers only the heart can hear.

Roman was never meant to stay. Rae was never meant to listen.

And yet here they are, tangled in a house that remembers every moan, every sin, every unfinished goodbye.

There's a man who won't let go. Another who doesn't know how.

And a woman caught between what's real... and what's *possessing* her.

This story aches. It shivers. It burns slow and deep and holy.

And if you're very, very lucky... it'll leave a mark on you, too.

Tell me, darling reader... would you dare let the dead claim you? Would you surrender your soul to the silence, the shadow, the promise of something more?

Would you become—

*Your Ghost's Possession?*

# CHAPTER ONE

The house is already watching us when we pull up.

Dusk spills long shadows across the gravel drive, and the last of the sun bleeds out behind the gabled roof, turning the windows to black mirrors. It might have been beautiful once—light stone, elegant lines—but time and rot have eaten it down to bone. Moss clings like mould. Ivy chokes the porch railings. Something unseen crawls beneath the surface.

Nate kills the engine, and silence settles like dust.

"Hell of a stereotype," I murmur.

He chuckles, but it sounds hollow.

Neither of us moves.

The quiet stretches.

Then I reach for the handle.

I open my door and slide to the gravel driveway with a crunch. I plant my hands on my hips and nod solemnly.

He slides open the side door of the van and starts hefting out bags and equipment. I would normally help, but I'm utterly transfixed. I stare up at the black windows, the peeling wooden frames around them, and the crooked slates on the even more crooked roof. In our line of work, we've seen some pretty run-down buildings, but this is right out of a horror movie. I take a step towards the house and a creeping sensation moves up my spine. I ignore it, used to such feelings, and keep walking slowly towards the house. A soft hum leaves my lips and my steps slow. It's getting harder to move closer, like walking through treacle.

"Rae?" Nate calls from the van. "Can you lend a hand?"

"Yeah," I reply absently, still taking laboured steps towards the porch.

The loud clang of something metal falling over snaps me out of it and I turn and stride around to Nate's side of the van. He's got out most of our things already and I offer him a sheepish smile.

"You getting something already?" He asks, glancing sideways at me as he slides one last plastic box out of the back of the van.

I nod, unsure how to put the sensation into words.

"Well," he says, jingling a set of keys. "Good job we're here."

We approach the steps up onto the porch, each with a bag on our backs and a box in our hands. That desperate melancholy, mixed with simmering fury overwhelms me again, pulling me in but simultaneously pushing me away. The spirit of this place wants desperately to be left alone.

"Nate," I whisper as we take the first steps up to the porch. "We need to be very careful with this one."

He doesn't reply, he simply glances my way and gives me a nod. The wood of the porch is old and creaks beneath our feet. I feel like a kid again, approaching the creepiest house in the neighbourhood on Halloween after being dared to knock on the door. It's not often I get this feeling. Not after the things I've seen and experienced. Not after nearly thirty years of seeing dead people.

Nate props the big box in his hands on one hip as he

shuffles through the keys and finds the one for the front door. It's not unusual for the owners of the properties we investigate to be absent. Often times they've already moved out, unable to cope any more with the disturbances. But this time, the owner has never even set foot in the house and refuses to do so until we, in his words "deal with it". He bought it at auction, site unseen, and the first time he came here he knew before he'd even gotten as far as we have, that there was a problem here. I suspected he was sensitive, like me, but unaware and untrained in dealing with hauntings himself. So he'd called us, desperate to be able to make good on his investment.

There's a jingle as Nate slides the key into the lock. The house groans and my gaze whips up to the sloped roof of the porch above us.

"We're not welcome."

"Yes we are," Nate says, calm and steady as ever. "The owner invited us here."

Ahh, Nate, my faithful, and faithless companion. He's not a believer. He's a... sceptic. There. I said it. He's my tech guy. He's fascinated by the paranormal but is adamant that there is a perfectly rational, scientific explanation for everything. I couldn't do this without him. He keeps me grounded. But he doesn't feel the things I feel. He hasn't seen the things I've seen. And because of that, there's always some distance between us, despite the fact that we travel together all over the country, spend endless hours together on cases and have had to share some pretty close quarters over the last few years. But we remain just good friends, and co-workers.

This job is the reason my marriage ended. Always on the road, always swept up in the cases that demand all of my emotional awareness. I had another partner before Nate and my ex-husband was jealous, even though that was entirely platonic too. It's hard to hold a relationship together under those circumstances. So here I am, almost forty and single. Living out of a van half the time and in crappy hotels in between hauntings the rest of the time. It doesn't even pay that well. But I can't do anything else. I'm called to it. And when I help a spirit to move on? Well, that's what makes it all worthwhile.

Nate gets the door unlocked and pushes it open with a heavy creak. He steps inside and tries the light switch inside the door. But nothing happens.

"Naturally," he mutters, stepping over the threshold. I follow him inside. Thick dust lines the wooden floorboards of the wide hallway. Stairs ahead of us lead up onto a high landing with a broken piece of banister. There are doors to our left and right and the hallway ahead leads to a kitchen at the back of the house.

Usually when we take a case, the owner is able to lay out a whole list of unexplained phenomena for us and there's always a pattern. But we know nothing about this one except that the owner was too terrified to open the front door from the moment he saw the place. I understand now exactly why.

The atmosphere is as thick as the build up of dust. It's clawing at my throat even now as I stand here in the hallway. Every fibre of my being is screaming at me to turn and RUN!

But I'm used to these messages and am able to ignore it. More or less.

Nate, on the other hand, is always completely ignorant of such messages. He's the least sensitive person I know, spiritually speaking, of course. He's a soft and lovable human being who cares about the living, he just has zero awareness of the dead. Lucky for him, I guess. But when I glance his way now, he looks pale. He cranes his neck to peer down the hall. He puts the box down and slides his bag off his shoulder to drop on the floor beside the box.

"I'll get lights from the van." He turns and vanishes out the door too quickly for me to reply.

That tells me everything I need to know.

I take a few tentative steps into the hall. I lean through the open door on the left into what must have been a parlour in some long-past time. There are chairs covered with dust sheets and badly worn curtains and rug in matching burgundy-turned-grey, thick dust over everything. The large object in front of the window, covered with a dust-grey sheet, can only be a piano.

The breeze from the open door blows the dust sheets and one of them billows up, sending dust reeling into the air. I step back and start to turn away when a shape in the swirling dust grabs my attention. There's a man standing right there by the fireplace. I step into the room and fix my keen eyes on where I saw him, but there's nothing there but dust, shimmering in the low light.

The room is ice-cold and my breath clouds in front of my lips.

Well, hello. The spirit has messed up, revealing himself to me so soon. Now I know that he knows what I am because I saw him and he knows it.

Nate's heavy footsteps on the wooden porch echo dully in the hall and there's a clatter as he deposits the equipment on the floor. I sweep the room one last time before turning and heading back into the hall.

I fix my steely gaze on Nate, who looks over at me with a frown.

"You okay?" he asks.

I nod. "Let's get started."

# CHAPTER TWO

The three bright spot lights on their stands shine their garish white light across the dusty, wooden floor of the house, the furniture casting deep, dark shadows in the path of the lights. We have one by the parlour window, one in the hall pointing towards the kitchen and another in what turned out to be the dining room opposite the parlour. All the doors are open so that the light can spill through the doorways.

"We'll head upstairs when we're done down here," I instruct as Nate finishes plugging in his instruments. The lights and all of our electronics are getting power from the portable generator we brought with us. Thank fuck we always come prepared.

The chill in the air has only intensified with the setting sun. I'm still in my coat, hat and gloves and Nate is similarly wrapped up. It shouldn't be this cold.

"Are we ready to record?"

"All systems are go," Nate says, patting his gloved hands together to warm them. He has microphones set up around the ground floor, all recording to his laptop and there are cameras on tripods near each of the lights. This is pretty standard for us. Nate once showed me the cupboard in his meagre flat filled with external hard drives full of all our recordings. He's methodical about record-keeping. Unlike me. I tend to rely too much on my memory, which is good, but makes mistakes.

I walk once more through the lit spaces, making a complete circuit of the ground floor. I go slowly, taking in the shifting energies of the space.

"It's coldest in here," I say as I re-enter the parlour. "And there's a spot right in front of the fireplace that's got something—off about it. I don't know what." I go and stand there and close my eyes. The fireplace is roughly boarded up and there's a flowing dust sheet over the chaise longue in front of it that wafts in the draught coming down the chimney. As I stand there, taking deep breaths, someone draws closer to me. But Nate is standing on the far side of the room. I'd have heard his footsteps on the wooden floor if he'd approached. He doesn't know how to be quiet.

The unmistakable sensation of crawling moves over my skin under my many layers. There's a question in the air.

"What do you want to ask?"

I'm met with silence so deafening a shudder runs up my spine. I don't spook easily. I right my shoulders and take another breath.

"We're here to help. If you talk to me then I can help you sooner."

A cool breath rushes over the back of my neck. I press my lips together and hold still. Another soft breath follows, audible in my ear. I crack one eye open a touch and lock my gaze onto Nate. He's watching me through the pop-out screen on the camera on the other side of the room, his head canted to one side and a deep frown etched into his brow.

"What are you seeing, Nate?" I ask, my voice barely above a whisper.

"I'm not sure. There's something—" He leans closer to the screen, squinting. "What are you feeling?"

"There's someone behind me. A man. He's curious. I'm not sensing any particular anger like I did when we arrived. He wants to communicate, I can feel it." I close my eyes again and lean into my other senses. "Talk to me. I'm listening."

Another breath brushes against my skin. Touch. That's the way in. I whip my hat off, followed by my gloves and I toss them onto the covered chaise longue. I unzip my padded coat and slip it off my shoulders, exposing more of my neck.

"What are you doing?" Nate asks, looking directly at me rather than through the video feed.

"He can communicate through touch."

"Right." He nods. He stops short of rolling his eyes. I snap my eyes shut again.

Icy fingers slither over my shoulder and across my collar bone. I gasp, but hold still and quiet. My back runs cold, like icy water is flowing down it. My breath quickens. A soft, low hum reverberates through my chest but I'm not making the sound.

*You are intriguing.*

My eyes ping open and fix on Nate. He looks from me to the video and back again, his mouth slightly open. He snaps it shut again and checks the microphone.

"You're intriguing too," I murmur, afraid to break the spell. "Can you speak to me now that you can touch my skin?"

*Hmm. Such pale, smooth skin. Alas, I cannot really touch it. But I can feeeeel it.*

It takes everything I have not to yell and run over to Nate. This is some next level communication. Normally I only get feelings, fleeting impressions, from a spirit. I feel cold spots in rooms, visceral moments of rage or fear. But only once before have I heard full sentences from a spirit. And that is an experience I try not to think about. Ever.

"What's your name?" My voice trembles and I hate that I'm showing fear.

*Roman. What's yours?*

"Hi, Roman. I'm Rae. This is my friend, Nate. He's recording us. Is that okay?"

*I don't understand those words. But my question is how can you see and hear me?*

"I'm a medium," I reply. "I can often communicate with spirits, like you. But not usually as clearly as this. Nate? Are you picking him up on the mic?"

Nate tilts his head side to side, still frowning. He has headphones on and is watching the screen of his laptop.

"I'm getting something, but it's not clear."

"Roman? Can you tell me what's keeping you here?"

*I was waiting for you, Rae.*

His voice is like silk under my skin. A shudder runs through my shoulders and my coat falls right down my arms and thuds to the floor. The cold on my back intensifies. His icy breath on the back of my neck does something to me that I'm ashamed to admit.

"I'm here now," I reply, my eyes closed and my head rocking back. My hair moves, as if fingers are slipping through the long, thick curls.

*Yes, thank goodness.*

"So what can I do for you, Roman? To help you move on?"

"Rae?" Nate's voice carries a question and a note of concern. I straighten my head and peer at him through narrowed eyes.

*Move on?* Roman asks.

"Rae?"

*Why on earth would I go anywhere when you just got*

*here?*

"Hmm? Why do you need me?" I ask, lost in my own strange thoughts.

"Rae." Nate's persistence niggles at me. But I only want to hear Roman.

*I just need you, Rae. I need all of you. You can hear me. I can't recall the last time anyone heard me. Or saw me. Or knew me. But you can. You can know me better.*

"What do you mean?"

"Rae!" Firm hands grasp my shoulders and shake me. My vision focuses on Nate. He's right in my face and I startle, almost pulling out of his grip. "This is really fucking strange, Rae. Snap out of it. Come on. Keep a clear head."

I nod and press my lips together. It is, indeed, very strange.

"Come look at this." He drags me by the arm over to his laptop. I can see the sound waves where he's been recording audio. I see the spikes where one of us spoke. But as we stand there in the quiet, the line is almost flat. Nate clicks the button to change the view so I can see more of the recording and in the gaps between the spikes of my own voice, there are other lines. Not the clear spikes of normal speech, but long, low waves.

*What are you looking at?* Roman asks. I watch the screen and see one of those thick lines form.

"It's picking him up, he just asked me what we're looking at."

"What the fuck?" Nate looks from the screen, to me, to where I was just standing.

"You're looking at proof, Nate."

*Proof? Proof of what, Rae?*

He's right behind me again and I leap sideways into Nate, knocking him into the camera tripod. It wobbles perilously, but his quick reflexes catch it.

"What?" He asks, his attention torn between the tripod and me.

"Sorry, Roman, the spirit, he's right here." I gesture the space the ghost is occupying.

"You're hearing speech, right? Full sentences?"

I nod, afraid to look away from the spot where Roman is standing. I can't see him, not exactly, but I sense him the same way I would sense a physical person standing close to me.

"That's different," Nate says, straightening the camera so that it points at where I indicated Roman's location.

"This is all different."

"I don't like it."

I'm about to say I don't like it either, but the words stick in my throat. It's not really true. I'm scared, sure, but there's something else too. Excitement. Curiosity. And that other thing that I can't face.

*Rae. I'd like to touch you. Would you allow it?*

"How would you do that?"

"Do what?" Nate asks, then realises I'm not talking to him. "This is fucking weird," he mutters.

My skin prickles and I glance down at my bare forearms where goosebumps are spreading across my skin. The slippery cold of melting ice oozes across my collarbones again. I'm fairly sure that this time, Roman is in front of me and is using both hands to trace the prominent shadows on my skin. The tendrils of cold slither up to my neck and I tilt my head back to expose more skin to him. I'm warming up, rather than cooling down, despite the frosty feel of his touch. Okay, I'll just admit it right now, this guy is turning me on.

"Rae?"

I want nothing more than for Nate to shut up.

"I'm fine. Everything's fine."

*Hmm. You are so warm. I need more. I need to feel you all over me.*

"Uh-huh." That's about the most coherent thing I can manage.

*So warm. So alive.*

The cold surrounds me, coating my entire upper body as if he's enveloping me. His breath flows over my face, my lips. Oh dear God. How is he doing this?

"Rae! That's enough. Rae." Nate's rough voice shakes me out of this… trance. His hands are on my upper arms again and his face is up close to mine. I right myself and a gush of warm fluid hits my top lip. Nate's eyes widen and my fingers dart to my mouth, where the metallic tang of blood is creeping between my lips.

Nate fishes in his pocket and presses a handkerchief to my nose and upper lip. "Your nose is bleeding."

"I gathered." I shoot him a scowl, but immediately soften and take the hanky into my own hand. I look around the room but there is no visible sign of what happened. "He's gone." I know it in my bones. The room is warmer and Roman's presence has slunk away.

"Gone, gone?" Nate asks, disbelieving.

"No. Just for now."

A crash breaks the eerie silence. We glance at each other then bolt for the door to the hall. Nothing. We run across the hall into the dining room and the light we'd set up in here to shine through to the kitchen is on its side, smashed and dark. Nate moves over to it and broken glass crunches under his heavy boot.

"I think we angered him." Nate looks back at me.

"Or you did." I catch another drip of blood from my nose with the handkerchief as I stare at the damaged light.

"Or I did." Nate echoes, nodding, his hands planted on his

hips. "Because I *pulled* you out of whatever that was. Rae, you were *gone*. Are you all right now?"

"Yeah, I'm fine."

"We should pack up and go to the hotel."

"Not a chance." I shake my head. "We need to stay here and see if anything else happens."

"Rae," Nate shakes his head. "That's not a good idea. This whole situation is strange. We've never experienced anything like this before. We need to regroup."

"No." I snap. I turn and head back into the hall, my gaze sweeps up the stairs, where a door softly closes. "We're staying right here. I can help him move on. I know I can."

Nate's scepticism takes on a new, savage tone as he follows me into the hall and stomps past me into the parlour. "Yeah, sure, or help him get off."

# CHAPTER THREE

In sullen silence, Nate and I move our equipment around to compensate for the shattered light. I'm stung by his words, but mainly because I know there's truth in them. He switches the cameras to record in night mode and sets the light in the parlour to the motion sensor so it doesn't run all night. I head up the stairs first, a torch in hand to guide me. I follow the landing to the left first and head to the front of the house.

The main bedroom would have been beautiful a few decades ago. In the centre of the room is a grand four-poster bed with intricate patterns engraved in the wood. An old and worn down-stuffed mattress lays bare and slightly off-centre. The bed hasn't been covered or cared for while the house stood empty and judging from the ragged hole in one corner and scattered feathers, some rodents have made a nest out of the mattress. I shudder and shine the torch beam around the rest of the room. There's a fireplace much like the one in the parlour below but this one isn't boarded up and a strong draught blows out of it. The windows are bare and there's a dark stain on the bare floorboards between the bed and the window.

Nate's heavy footsteps approach along the landing and he

peers into the room around me.

"Nice." His one word sums it all up in his delivery.

"Yeah. Let's not sleep in here." I step back into the hall and close the door with a firm click.

"What are the rest of the rooms like?" He asks.

We move around the upper floor, examining what we've got. The bedroom behind the main one is relatively hospitable. Twin beds stand at right-angles to each other and have been covered with heavy-duty dust sheets. Under the sheets are decent mattresses and even some intact, if musty, linens. The bathroom is next to this room, directly over the kitchen. Despite the lack of power, we have running water. Of sorts. It runs brown and smells of sulphur, but the toilet flushes and I cling to that fact. It's one of those old toilets with a cistern mounted high on the wall above the bowl and flushes with a chain with a vaguely phallic wooden handle on the end.

"Let's not drink the water," Nate suggests and I nod in agreement.

The other bedroom is in a similar state to the main one, only with no bed at all and a hole in the floorboards under the window—which is also smashed in with broken glass scattered across the floor. We close that door as well and make our way to the final room at the front of the house, above the dining room. It was once a study, although the floor-to-ceiling mahogany bookcases are all empty and coated in dust. A large matching desk sits in the corner opposite the door between windows on the front and side of the house.

The most interesting thing in the room, however, is what's hidden under another large dust sheet. Nate yanks it off with a flourish that scatters dust into the air. A selection of huge canvas prints is propped up against the bookshelves and we carefully drag them out to prop up around the room so we can examine them.

"Wow." Nate exhales as we shine the torch light over the oil paintings. Five of them feature the same woman in states of increasing undress. The first depicts her in Victorian horse-riding gear complete with veiled hat and riding crop, but the top few buttons of her jacket are undone, scandalously exposing her neck and a sheen on her face suggests she was sweating. In the next one, she's reclining on a chaise longue with bare feet and her long skirt hitched up to expose her knees. She's fanning herself and has an unmistakable glint in her eye that tells me she was hot for her portrait-painter.

"It's you." Nate's voice cuts through the eerie silence.

"Don't be daft."

But I look again at each of the paintings. She has long, reddish-brown hair in thick curls like mine, and the shape of her lips is similar to mine. Her figure is even close to my own. "Huh."

By the fifth time she sat for him, she was naked. Her head is thrown back, her hair cascading down behind her. One hand is on her breast, the other is touching herself between her thighs. Heat rises in my cheeks and I can't help hoping that I look that hot when I'm masturbating.

The final painting is the most debauched. It shows not just her, but several naked people. Two men are fucking over a card-table in the background. On the other side of the painting is a straight couple engaged in something I can only describe as carnal. The woman from the other portraits is reclined on her chaise longue again but this time, another woman is eating her out and her eyes are focused directly on us. Or rather, whoever painted this scene.

"Is that the parlour downstairs?" Nate asks, the beam of his torch lingering on the orgy scene.

"I think so. Look." I touch the fireplace in the background

of the painting. "That's the same fireplace. And I'll bet you anything if we remove the dust sheet from that piece of furniture in front of the fire it's this chaise longue."

"Agreed." He shuffles his feet and moves the torchlight away, but my gaze lingers on the scene. I'm feeling distinctly more warm than I have any right to be in a cold and dusty old house full of holes.

After setting up the other light and camera on the landing, again with motion detectors set up to trigger them, we head into the one decent bedroom and Nate sets his backpack down next to the bed nearest the door. He unrolls his sleeping bag onto the bed and I do the same. There may be bedding on these beds, but it's old and smells funky.

Nate and I have shared a room more times than I can count, but we still always turn our backs to one another to change. I put my boots by the bed unlaced and ready to put on in a hurry. I take my jeans off and fold them up at the end of the bed. I slide into my sleeping bag in my knickers and t-shirt and glance over at Nate. He's stripped down to his boxers and t-shirt and has set himself up the same way that I have. It's a habit at this point. My gaze lingers on his muscular thighs a moment too long.

If things were different, maybe there'd be more than friendship there. He's a good-looking guy. Sandy hair, sexy stubble and an athletic body. But his scepticism is a barrier. I know, deep down, that no matter how jovial and thoughtful he is, he believes I'm not really psychic. He's looking for a way to prove that there's some other explanation for everything I've spent my life experiencing. That one thing keeps a barrier between us that can't be ignored.

"Night," he says softly from across the room.

"Night." I listen to him settle down in the pitch black. I'm not ready to sleep yet. I always stay awake later than him so I can spend some time alone with the energy of the place we're investigating. I rest my head against the wall and close my eyes. Frustration niggles at me as I sit there. I'm annoyed with Nate and even more so with myself. I don't know what came over me downstairs. I just know that there's something different about this case, this spirit. He's getting inside my head in a way no other spirit has.

My thoughts drift back to the paintings, to the woman in them and particularly the orgy. I never do any research on our cases before we visit the locations. I don't want the history to influence what I pick up. It's one way I ensure my integrity. But Nate does. He digs up everything he can on the locations before we ever set foot in them. He likes to be prepared and to verify what I pick up. He hasn't mentioned anything yet and I know he won't until we've been here longer. He holds back as much as possible in the name of not tainting the results. I wonder if he found anything about a former resident here being a painter, or holding orgies.

I imagine myself in that painting, looking past the woman between my thighs at the man painting me. My left hand idly caresses my breast, my thumb rubbing gently back and forth over my nipple through my t-shirt. My right hand rests on the gentle curve of my belly. My fingers carefully inch under the elastic of my underwear.

Nate shifts his weight and takes a heavy breath that halts my movements. I lay still, my eyes open wide. Is it just me, or has the room gotten colder since I got into my sleeping bag? I reach out with my senses and release a shaking breath that clouds lightly in front of my lips.

*Go on. Touch yourself.*

The voice is deep and sonorous. It makes my bones vibrate.

I do as Roman commands and resume caressing my nipple and moving my right hand deeper. I part my moist labia and run my fingers either side of my clitoris. I sweep my fingers back up and over the hard bud of flesh. I pinch my lower lip between my teeth and try to breathe normally.

*That's good. Again.*

I rub my middle finger around my clit and over it again. And again. My breathing quickens.

*Very nice.*

My skin breaks out in goosebumps. Cold seeps through my sleeping bag and under my skin.

I move my fingers lower and slide them inside my wet pussy.

*Hmm yes. I like that.*

Icy cold caresses my lips and they part slightly to release a shuddering breath. Roman surrounds me, engulfing me in his cold energy.

*I want to be inside you, my Dove. Devouring you from within.*

A whimper escapes my parted lips. My fingers move slowly back and forth over my g-spot, rubbing the smooth nub inside me. The heel of my thumb presses against my clitoris, firmly stimulating that sensitive spot. My thoughts return to the paintings. I picture the one of the woman on her own, pleasuring herself like this. I wonder if he got off on this in life as in death.

*I do like to watch*, he says softly in my ear.

So he can read my thoughts. I return them to the orgy painting.

*My favourite. There's something extra special in the paint, my Dove.*

Eww. I don't linger on that thought. I wonder who the woman was.

*The love of my life. And my ruin.*

Interesting choice of words. But I'm losing coherence in my thoughts now. I slip my fingers out of my pussy and return them to my tender clit, rubbing more quickly now to compensate for the lack of friction now that my fingers are soaked in my own fluids. My breath comes in soft and broken gasps as my pleasure mounts.

If this guy was alive, I'd fuck him right now. Jesus. I'm so turned on. I've never had sex with a stranger before, but I'd make an exception for this seductive spirit.

*Yes, Dove. I would pleasure you for hours on end. I would make you come hard before finishing in you. I wouldn't let you sleep for a moment. If I had a body.*

A shaky whimper escapes my mouth as I come, imagining him fucking me even though I don't know what he looked like. I hold my breath, suddenly aware that I'm not alone. I hold still and listen, A soft, rhythmic rustling of nylon fabric comes from Nate's bed followed by an almost inaudible gasp as he comes.

I withdraw my fingers and wipe them on my t-shirt as I struggle to settle my breathing down. Knowing that he was jerking off to the sound of me doing the same threatens to turn me on even more. I turn my head in his direction and consider what it might mean for our friendship.

I lie in the dark, my breath soft and unsteady. Roman's touch is gone, but I can still feel him—like frost on my skin, like shadow in my lungs.

Across the room, Nate doesn't speak—but I know he's awake. I can feel it in the weight of the silence between us. I turn onto my side and pull the sleeping bag tighter around me, trying to trap the warmth, trying to calm my racing heart. But I already know sleep won't come. A shiver moves through me, not from the cold. From something deeper.

*Soon*, Roman whispers, just a breath against my ear.

And I realise—with a pulse of fear and longing—I don't want him to stop.

# CHAPTER FOUR

My sleep is fitful, but at least I get some. At one point, I think I can hear the faint tinkling of piano keys but I chalk it up to my edginess and go back to sleep.

The grey light of dawn wakes me. Nate is already dressed and gone from the room, and his sleeping bag is fully unzipped and laying open to air it out. I do the same and tiptoe to the bare window, my arms hugging myself. There are trees pressing close to the house and their bare branches scratch lightly against the sloping roof of the porch below the window.

"Oh, hi." Nate's voice breaks the silence. I turn around, suddenly self-conscious as I stand there in just my t-shirt and underwear. He stands in the doorway holding his toiletry bag. His gaze rakes swiftly over all of my exposed skin before he turns away and puts his toiletries back in his bag.

"Did you sleep okay?" I ask as I scurry back to my things and pick up my jeans.

"Fine, thanks. Eventually."

I halt with one leg in my jeans. His back is to me and he's hunched over his bag, but he's still too.

"Same." I finally reply and resume getting dressed. "We

should check the recordings, see if anything got picked up over night."

"Yeah. I'm on my way down to pack up the laptop. I'm taking you to that café down by the main road for breakfast. We need to get out of here for a while."

"Agreed. I need to get warm." A slight smile quirks my lips and our eyes meet.

"See you downstairs." He sweeps from the room and pulls the door part way closed behind him. I watch him go, my pulse racing. There's so much unsaid.

After breakfast and an hour away from the house, the chill has faded from my bones—but not from my mind. Roman hasn't made another appearance, but I feel his absence like a hollow space carved in my chest. I try not to think about the way he touched me. The way I let him.

Back at the house, Nate and I move quietly, checking cameras and transferring data. Neither of us mentions the sounds we heard in the night. Not the whisper that wasn't mine. Not the rustling fabric. Not the muffled gasps.

We review the footage in the study, back among the dust sheets and decadence. The orgy painting still sits propped against the bookcase, watching us.

Nothing conclusive shows on the camera feeds—just shifting shadows, low frequency spikes on the audio, a cold spot that drifts in and out of the parlour.

But I feel him.

Waiting.

By the time the sun sets again, the tension between Nate and I is unbearable. I've caught him looking at me more than once—really looking. And I'm no better. His jaw when he clenches it. His hands when he tightens the straps on a case. The memory of his soft gasp in the night plays on loop in my mind, stirring something wicked inside me.

"Same room tonight?" he asks after a dinner of take-out pizza and ice cream, though it's not really a question.

I nod. "Of course."

He doesn't look at me as he climbs the stairs.

We set up just like before. Twin beds. Sleeping bags. Layers of clothes and silence between us. But it feels different now. Like we're pretending we haven't already touched each other in the dark—through distance, through imagination, through a ghost.

I lie back and let the quiet stretch long between us.

It doesn't take long.

The cold starts at my feet this time. Slipping inside the sleeping bag. Up the backs of my calves. Over the swell of my thighs.

My body arches, breath catching.

*You feel me, don't you, Dove?*

I close my eyes and nod.

*Good. Tonight, I want more.*

I catch my lip between my teeth and wait, listening intently. Nate is absolutely silent, not even his breathing makes a sound. That's how I know he's awake and waiting too.

Roman's presence seeps under my skin and chills me deep inside. I brace myself, tensing against the cold. The lightest touch brushes over my thighs, icier than the pervasive cold. His spectral fingers tingle against my skin.

My thumbs move the elastic around my hips and hook under it. I shimmy awkwardly out of my underwear and leave it balled up in the bottom of my sleeping bag.

*That's better.*

A silky hum makes its way up from my knees, the cold moving with it. I part my legs and the cold intensifies right over my entrance. I slide a finger slowly into it and hold my breath.

I'm still upholding the pretence of secrecy. I keep as quiet as possible as I begin to work my finger inside me. Roman's cold touch slithers inside me, joining my hand. A gasp escapes my parted lips.

*Yes, Dove. I want you to come.*

Me too. God. I need more.

*I wish I could be with you fully. I want you so deeply.*

I can feel his passion oozing off him and wonder what it would have been like to be with him in life. I'm betting it would have been sizzling heat, not this frigid cold.

*I could show you.*

I slow my pulsing hand and wait for him to elaborate.

*I could show you a memory if you let me into your mind fully. You're still holding back, Dove.*

He's right, of course. I have firm walls around my mind to protect me from the spirits I work with. Even with him I'm keeping something back, something locked away behind those walls. The very essence of me. What he's proposing is dangerous. He's talking about possession. If I let down my walls and take him fully into me, I could be inviting him to stay forever. I could lose myself.

It's no small thing he's asking.

I realise my hand has stopped, but the gentle rustling from Nate's sleeping bag tells me I haven't been as quiet as I intended. I resume stroking myself as I consider Roman's offer. I really want to see what he wants to show me. But how can I trust him?

*Have I hurt you or your friend?*

Well, no. Not at all.

*I'm not going to harm you, Dove. I want to pleasure you.*

I slip my finger out and rub it over my clit. All right. I want to see.

I'm plunged into a deep, psychic pool of icy water and gasp

for breath as I sink into it. The water rushes into my lungs and freezes me from inside. But just as my vision begins to fade to black, it clears and I'm lying on the chaise longue from the portraits in front of a roaring fire. The woman from the portraits stands by the fire, naked, her hands on her round hips. I'm seeing her from Roman's eyes. This is his memory.

"You are beauty itself," he says. She smiles and bats her eyelashes. She speaks but I don't hear her words. He moves towards her and places his hands on either side of her face. His lips press against hers, warm and smooth. I am both him and her, feeling all of their emotions and each physical touch. It's overwhelming. I'm coming already, even though they aren't having sex yet. My own hand is working hard on my clit and I'm groaning. My body is in the dusty bedroom, two meters from Nate, but my mind is a hundred years in the past in the warm parlour.

Roman scoops the woman into his arms and spins her around. He runs his hands up her arms and places her hands on the warm wood of the head-height mantle. She gasps, or I do, I'm not sure which, as Roman thrusts into her from behind. He holds her hips tight as he thrusts, taking long, slow and deep motions. I am both voyeur and participant in this intense psychic phenomenon unlike anything I've ever experienced before.

My real body shudders and cries out.

Roman fucks his lover and me all at once. Sweat beads on my forehead from the fire. My naked breasts sway with the gentle rocking of our bodies and my pale skin glows in the orange firelight.

"Oh god," I gasp. "Yes. More."

Roman picks up the pace and pumps harder and faster. My hand stimulates my clit vigorously in time with his thrusts.

Sudden cold rushes over my body and I'm ripped out of the

memory and into my own body. Firm hands grasp my shoulders and Nate's lips call my name mutely right in my face. I'm confused, shaken and reeling from my orgasm.

"What? What are you doing? Where am I?" My cum-soaked fingers grip Nate's bulging bicep and my eyes struggle to focus in the dark.

"Rae? Can you hear me?"

"Yes. I can hear you." I spit angrily, tugging out of his grasp. "Why did you pull me out?"

"Because you were gone! The lights were on but there was no one home. Where did he take you?" He's kneeling on the bed, still too close to me. I pull back, pressing myself against the wall at the head of the bed. My head shakes. My whole body is trembling uncontrollably. I can't speak. I can't admit what I did. He moves back and huffs. His head turns away and he leans forward, resting his elbows on his knees.

Fuck. I'm still craving more. Sexually charged to a thousand volts.

"Nate," I whisper, moving towards him. An idea taking root. "I'm sorry. I was in a memory of him and his lover. He took me there. I was lost. Thank you. You pulled me back. I might have got stuck there." I know full well a part of me is still locked there, on pause, waiting for Roman to hit play again. The spirit's icy tendrils still curl under my scalp. I run a hand over Nate's shoulder and he turns to look at me. His breath is warm on my face.

I'm completely out of my sleeping bag now and crawling into Nate's lap. He lets me. He invites me. His hands take hold of my hips. "You saved me," I whisper, my lips brushing over his.

His hands tighten on my hips and his eyes roam over my lips in the dark. The only light coming from the light on the landing shining under the door. Nate's cock twitches through his boxers.

*Yes. Roman's silky voice slides through my mind. We can be together like this. I can be inside you through him.*

I reach between us and tug Nate's erection out of his pants. I ease myself down onto him, taking him into me with a sigh.

Roman sighs too. So does Nate. The three of us are connected now. I feel both of them in me. Nate physically, Roman psychically. A long whimper rushes out of my mouth.

I roll my hips, moving on Nate and him moving in me. His hands move up from my hips. Sliding under my t-shirt. His thumbs brush over my hard nipples. I lift my arms and he pulls my top up over my head. He grabs both of my breasts firmly in his hands and sinks his mouth onto the left one. His breath is hot, his mouth hotter.

The slick, slithering cold of Roman's presence moves around from my spine to where Nate and I are joined.

Nate gasps, feeling the cold too. It seeps into my pussy, chilling me inside.

"What the fuck?" Nate gasps, holding me still.

"Let me fuck you, Nate. Please."

He nods uncertainly and plants his mouth on mine, kissing me deeply.

I resume rocking my hips, grinding against him. I moan into his mouth and wrap my hands around the back of his neck. He knows Roman is in the mix, he has to. But he kisses me with passion and thirst, his hands clamp onto my butt and help to keep me rocking as my climax rushes through me. My pussy clenches around his cock and I feel every throb of his pulse inside me.

The ghost moans inside my head and the cold of his touch inside my body and soul makes me shudder. I feel the moment he climaxes. There's no physicality to it, but the intensity of his feeling rushes through me.

A moment later, Nate's cock swells and he groans as he comes hard inside me.

We writhe together as we ride out our orgasms. All three of us. I feel Roman's spectral hands on my shoulders and his cold breath against the back of my neck. Another ripple of pleasure passes through me. My head tips back and a cry bursts from my throat.

Nate's penis twitches, his hands squeeze my backside and his lips press tender kisses to my breasts.

Roman swells inside me, filling me with his cold passion. I'm coming again, unable to stop.

Finally, slowly, I come down from the incredible high and come face to face with Nate. His blue eyes are fixed on me, his expression a mingling of desire and concern. Before he can ask what just happened, I kiss him, deeply, passionately.

Roman is still there, in me, around me, but silent. I don't need to hear his voice to know what he's thinking. What I'm thinking too: *This is just the beginning.*

# CHAPTER FIVE

I carefully ease myself off Nate's lap and stagger backwards on shaking legs. Our eyes don't quite meet. Shame starts to curl up from deep inside me. I used him. I wanted Roman and Nate was a proxy. Does he know that?

"Rae? Are you all right?"

"Umm…" A deep frown furrows my brow. That sickly feeling is moving up my throat. My stomach churns unpleasantly. My eyes widen and I clamp a hand over my mouth as I bolt for the bathroom. I just make it in time. Dinner exits my body into the toilet. My hands are planted on the grimy tiles, my arms shaking.

Nate is right behind me and scoops up my hair to hold it out of my face. His other hand rubs my back as I dry heave. Tears streak down my cheeks.

"I'm sorry," I mutter between coughs.

"What for?" His voice is soft and kind.

I wipe my mouth with the back of my hand and reach for the chain to flush the toilet. The plumbing groans in complaint, but the water runs and washes away my vomit. I turn to face Nate, shivering in the cold and he pulls me into his arms. "Hey, it's okay."

"No it isn't. That wasn't right."

"It was Roman, wasn't it?"

I nod against his firm chest, my tears staining his t-shirt.

He gently pulls away from me but keeps hold of my shoulders and ducks his head to look me in the eye. "I knew. I could tell you weren't yourself and I let it happen. If there's any blame to dish out, hand some to me. Okay?"

"Okay."

"Come on, we're getting out of here."

He leads me back to the bedroom and hurriedly gets dressed. I slowly go through the motions of dressing myself. I'm still only half done as he rolls up his sleeping bag. He finishes his and rushes over to do mine. I toss my things into my bag and hoist it onto my shoulder.

"Where are we going? It's the middle of the night."

"Just away. It doesn't matter."

"We can't abandon the job."

"We're not. We're taking care of you so you can finish it." He hoists his bag onto his shoulder and grabs both sleeping bags by their straps in one hand and takes my hand in his other. We hurry towards the stairs and the bedroom door slams behind us. I startle and my head whips around to look at the door. Nate doesn't hesitate, he leads me onto the stairs. We scurry down them and the broken piece of banister up on the landing drops with a crack on the step just behind me. I cry out and leap down the last two steps. Nate leads us out of the house and doesn't even lock up. We jump into the van and speed away with tyres slipping on the loose gravel.

We drive back to the café where we had breakfast and Nate pulls the van into the empty car park just off the road. The short parade of shops stands dark and still in the dead of night. Neither of us says a word. My tears have dried on my face and dust clings to my skin under my clothes. After a few deep breaths, Nate unbuckles his seat belt and reaches into the footwell on my side of the van to retrieve the hastily-stowed sleeping bags. He tosses them between us into the back of the van and climbs through after them. Slowly, my body aching, I follow him.

He unzips both bags and then fastens them together, making one double-sized bag. He shimmies down inside it and looks up at me, standing with my head and shoulders hunched against the roof of the van.

"Get in. It's freezing."

I kick my boots off and ease myself down into the bag beside him. I turn away from him, still racked with guilt about using him. But he won't let me lie in it alone. He pulls my back up against his chest and wraps his arms around me.

A fresh round of tears fall silently down my cheeks at his tenderness. I don't deserve this.

The sleeping bag does little to keep out the cold. It's not the kind of chill that can be fought with body heat and layers—it's the kind that gets in your bones, where guilt and regret live. Nate's arms stay around me all night, but neither of us sleeps much. I listen to his breathing change, settle, hitch again. I feel him twitch when I shift slightly, and once, his hand grazes mine and he flinches like I've burned him. Maybe I have.

The night passes slowly. Shadows stretch across the roof of the van, ghostly shapes cast by passing clouds and moonlight. Roman is silent now, but I still feel him. Lingering. Watching. Waiting. I shouldn't be able to feel him this far from the house. But I let him inside me and a part of him clings to me.

By morning, the windows are fogged from our breath. Nate stirs and pulls away first, sitting up and rubbing his face with both hands. His voice is rough when he speaks.

"Let's get some coffee."

We climb out of the van stiff and sore, the world washed in grey light and silence. The café opens early, a small miracle in our battered world, and we find ourselves at a table by the window, clutching hot mugs like they're lifelines. Neither of us has the appetite to eat, but we order out of habit—scrambled eggs, toast, something with mushrooms that neither of us touches.

The silence between us stretches, heavy and taut. I want to say something—apologise, explain, anything—but my throat is tight. I don't know how to talk about last night without falling apart.

Finally, Nate breaks the silence.

"So..." He stares into his coffee, then flicks a glance up at me. "Was it... him? Again?"

I nod slowly. "Yes. But it was different this time. He—he showed me something. A memory. It was like I was inside him, inside her... like I was both of them at once." I grip my mug tighter. "I didn't know that could even happen."

Nate doesn't respond right away. His jaw works, his fingers tightening around his cup. "And what about me?" he asks, voice low. "Was I just a... conduit?"

I wince. "No. I needed something real. And I—I took that from you."

He nods again, jaw clenched. "Okay."

Not "it's okay". Just "okay".

The silence that follows isn't quite forgiveness. But it's not rejection either. It's something in-between. And maybe that's where we'll have to live for now.

"Nate," I reach across the table for his hand, but he slides it out of reach. "I'm really sorry."

He takes a breath and glances around the quiet café. There is one other customer and the woman behind the counter. The coffee machine gurgles away and noises from the kitchen spill out, but it's quiet enough for our conversation to be overheard. Nate leans close and I lean in to meet him.

"You let him possess you. Right? That's how he showed you a memory?"

All I can do is nod. My throat feels hard and dry.

"Are you mad?" His voice is low and dangerous.

"It was a calculated risk. To try and find a way to reach him so I can do the job we were hired to do." There's more snap to my voice than I'd like. Maybe because of the guilt. Maybe because I know it was wrong.

"Sure," Nate snaps back, pulling away from me.

"Come off it. You don't even really believe anyway." I sit back in my chair and cross my arms. My eyes begin to tear up and I swiftly avert my gaze to the world outside the window.

"Is that what you think?" Nate's voice is quiet, stung. I return my gaze to him and a tear runs down my cheek. I swat it away and shift my weight.

"You're a sceptic. You always have been. You don't really think I can do what I do."

"Maybe at first, but after everything we've seen and done…" He shakes his head and clucks his tongue. "And if I had any doubts left, last night removed them. I felt him. He wasn't just in you, Rae."

"Oh." I falter. I lean closer. "What did you feel?"

"Cold. In places that shouldn't have been cold." His cheeks flush, showing up his light freckles. "And in my thoughts. And then there was the banister as we left. I don't have an explanation for that."

I nod and try again to take his hand. This time he lets me. A shaking breath rushes from my lips.

"I think we've both been influenced by him. I'm sorry for

my part in it all. I opened the door."

"You did. But I don't blame you for it. As for last night, I knew what was happening and I let it. So don't carry the weight of it on your own. Come on. Finish up. I'll pay and we'll go back. We have to collect our things before we go home."

"Home?" I pull away and a frown creases my brow. "We can't leave."

Nate is on his feet and feeling for his wallet in his back pocket. He stops and looks down at me.

"We need to."

"No, we have a job to do." Sure, I'm thinking about the money, but I'd be lying if I said that's all it was. I know that I'll always carry a piece of Roman with me if I don't help him to move on before I leave. I don't want that.

"Are you sure?"

"I am. It's important. I'll be more careful, I promise."

Nate doesn't speak. He turns and heads for the counter to pay. I grab the last half slice of toast and shove it into my mouth. A strange sense of relief ripples through me with the thought of going back to the house. I don't want to examine that too closely.

We ride in silence, the hum of the van and the rumble of tyres on tarmac the only sounds between us. The sun has fully risen now, casting a weak wash of gold over the frost-bitten fields. My stomach is still knotted, but at least there's something in it now. I press my forehead to the cool glass of the passenger window and watch as trees blur past, my breath leaving little ghosts on the glass.

Nate's grip on the wheel is tight. His knuckles are pale. He hasn't said a word since we left the café. I don't know if he's angry or just thinking. Maybe both.

When the house comes into view, it's like a pressure builds behind my eyes. My heart kicks up. The windows are still dark, still hollow. The broken railing on the porch hasn't fixed itself overnight. But it feels different. Expectant. As if it knew we'd come back.

As Nate pulls the van into the drive, he sighs. "Well," he says flatly, "home sweet home."

I want to reply with something light, something that will ease the tension between us. But all I can manage is a nod.

Because the truth is, I missed him. Roman. I shouldn't have. But I did.

And I think we all know it.

# CHAPTER SIX

The moment we step back over the threshold, the cold returns—not the lingering chill of winter air, but something deeper. Intentional. I feel it wrap around my ankles like invisible chains, tugging gently, insistently. The house is quiet, but it doesn't feel empty. If anything, it feels more alert. Like it's been waiting.

Nate's hand brushes mine as we walk through the hall, and I glance at him. His mouth is a hard line, his gaze fixed ahead. We don't speak.

The dust on the floor looks disturbed—more than just the marks we left behind. It's subtle, but my trained eyes catch the changes. A scuff here. A smudge there. Something—or someone—has been moving through the house.

We head for the stairs, stepping carefully over the broken piece of banister still lying on the steps. The doors upstairs remain closed, but one—the study—has been left ajar. My pulse skips.

We reach it together, Nate pushing the door open fully.

I stop cold.

All five paintings that had been propped so carefully against the bookcases now lie on the floor, some face-down, others leaning at awkward angles as though they'd been knocked over violently. Dust clings to the canvas edges like ash. But it's the largest painting—the orgy scene—that steals my breath.

It's still upright, but only just. Propped against the wall by the fireplace, the canvas is slashed through the centre, torn from top to bottom in jagged strokes. A letter opener—the antique kind, ornate and sharpened to a wicked point—is embedded in the floorboards at its base. One edge of the blade gleams red with old paint. Or something that might be paint.

My throat tightens. "He destroyed it."

Nate crouches beside the wreckage. "Why this one?"

I already know. The image had haunted me since we found it. Roman had shown me that scene in my mind—as if it had belonged to him. As if he'd created it. Claimed it. And then I'd given myself to someone else right beside it.

"He's angry," I say quietly. "Jealous, maybe. Or ashamed."

"Or unravelling," Nate mutters.

I walk slowly around the fallen canvases, careful not to step on them. The woman in the portraits—the one who looks like me—stares up at me from where she lies sideways in torn lace and soft shadows. Her painted eyes no longer meet mine. There's a rip through her throat in one of them.

Goosebumps prick my skin. Roman hasn't just made a mess. He's sent a message.

We don't speak for a while.

Nate moves the ruined paintings gently aside, lining them up against the bookcase with a care that borders on reverence. I perch on the edge of the desk, arms folded tight across my chest, watching him. Watching the jagged tear in the orgy painting. Roman didn't just destroy an image—he destroyed a mirror. A reflection of what we'd done. What I'd let happen.

Eventually, Nate straightens. His eyes are tired. Guarded. But underneath the frustration, I see something else. Worry. For me.

"Are you sure about this?" he asks. "About staying?"

I nod.

"Even after everything?"

"Yes." My voice is quiet, but certain. "We're closer than ever to understanding him. And I… I can't leave it like this."

He looks away, jaw flexing.

I know what he wants to say. That I'm not doing this for the job. That it's not just about helping Roman move on. That I've already let him in too far. That maybe I want more of what happened last night. And that part of him wants more of it too, even if he won't admit it.

But he doesn't say any of that.

Instead, he runs a hand through his hair and exhales slowly. "Then we stay."

He doesn't smile. Doesn't touch me. But the way he glances at me as he heads for the door tells me everything.

He's not just staying for the job either.

Nate closes the study door a little too firmly, the echo chasing us down the hallway. The silence between us stretches long and taut.

"I think we should get back to basics," he says eventually. "Start tracking like we usually do. Baseline temperature readings, motion sensors, EVP. The whole lot."

I nod, though my body's still buzzing from what we just saw. "Yeah. You're right."

But even as I say it, part of me knows I'm just agreeing to keep the peace. Roman's presence still lingers like perfume on the air—intangible but unmistakable. And a small, dangerous part of me doesn't want to sweep him out with cold spots and EM spikes.

Nate watches me for a moment longer, like he's waiting for more. When I don't say anything, he turns and heads down the stairs toward the equipment bags. I follow, slower, my fingertips grazing the old wallpaper as I pass.

We work in near silence. Nate checks cables, resets batteries, methodically lays out gear across the parlour and landing like a ritual he knows by heart. I help, but I'm going through the motions. I place sensors in corners without noting airflow. I jot times without logging temperature. My mind keeps drifting—to the woman in the paintings, to the letter opener, to the moment Roman sighed into my soul like he belonged there.

"You're not logging the EVP timestamps," Nate says quietly, not looking at me.

I blink down at the notebook in my hand, realising he's right. I flip the page and try again.

"I'm trying," I murmur.

"I know," he says. And there's something in his voice I can't quite place—not annoyance. Not even frustration. Just a quiet resignation. Like he knows I'm here, but only halfway.

When I glance over at him, he's already looking at me. His gaze drops almost instantly, back to the microphone he's setting up, but the heat of it lingers.

He wants to say something. I can feel it. But instead, he busies himself with wires and plugs and blinking lights, and the silence thickens around us once more.

We split up to place the motion sensors and thermometers —Nate downstairs, me upstairs. I try to focus. Really, I do. But the house feels thick with presence, like breathing soup. Every floorboard creak beneath my boots echoes louder than it should. Every shadow feels like it's watching.

When I return to the parlour, Nate is crouched by the

camera setup, staring at the display screen. He doesn't look up.

"I just reset this."

"What's wrong?"

"Sensor three keeps blinking off. But the power's fine. Battery's full. It's like... something's interfering."

"Could be the wiring."

He glances at me. "There's no wiring. They're wireless."

I move toward the camera, leaning to look, but the monitor fizzles with static before I can make anything out.

Nate sighs and leans back on his heels. "Of course. Perfect timing."

I try to suppress the shiver curling up my spine. "Try another channel."

He toggles through the feed. Camera four—parlour corner—flicks on, shows Nate and I frozen in black-and-white stillness.

And then the camera slowly tilts. A smooth, graceful motion. Not knocked. Not bumped. Tilted. We both stare.

"Did you see that?" I whisper.

Nate is already on his feet, crossing to the tripod. He inspects it, frowns, adjusts it back. "Could be a fault in the gimbal. Or the floor's uneven."

I don't respond. Behind him, the temperature sensor lets out a single beep. The cold spot.

He turns, following the sound. I remain where I am, acutely aware of the chill that's settled just beneath my skin. I can feel Roman now—not intense, not overwhelming. Playful. Whatever anger he felt at our leaving in the night, it's gone. We came back and now he's going to enjoy us. I shudder. Not with cold, not with revulsion, with deep anticipation.

The next monitor flicks to life on its own.

The camera angle is skewed slightly, but visible: me, standing still. Behind me, a breath of movement. Curtains flutter, though the window is closed.

Nate turns just in time to see the motion sensor flash red, then green, then red again. A rhythm.

My breath hitches. It's not a malfunction. It's a pulse. A heartbeat.

"Okay, what the fuck is going on?" Nate moves toward the equipment with growing agitation. "None of this makes sense."

I hug myself. Roman's here. He's teasing. Testing. Watching how I'll react—and how Nate will.

"Is this you? Did you make a mistake setting this up?"

"No," I snap, hugging myself tighter. "Of course not."

A pause. A heartbeat. Nate studies my face then heaves a sigh. He tilts his head to the ceiling and closes his eyes. When he straightens his head, his gaze flickers across my skin.

"Do you think it's him?" he asks. He's trying to stay calm, but I can hear the strain in his voice.

"Yes."

He swipes a hand over his face and laughs bitterly. "Great. So what's next? You want to ask him nicely to stop playing with the gear and ravish you again?"

I freeze.

He hears it as soon as he says it. His shoulders drop. "Shit. Sorry. That wasn't fair."

"No. It wasn't."

A long pause stretches between us. His hand hovers over a switch, but he doesn't flip it. Doesn't move.

"Did you like it?" he asks finally. Voice low. Rough. Not quite angry. Not quite curious. Something in between.

"I don't know," I whisper. "It felt like him. But it also felt like me."

Nate's eyes burn into mine across the room, his chest rising and falling like he's just run a mile.

The motion sensor beeps again—once, sharply. Then again. Again. Faster. The lights on the monitoring rig flicker. Nate turns toward it, but I see his hands shake. He knows what this is.

Roman's here. Pushing us. Testing how far he can make us fall.

I cross the room slowly. Every step crackles with tension, like walking through static. I'm burning inside. Tightness throughout my muscles. Arousal in my veins.

"Nate."

He doesn't look at me. His fists clench at his sides. He feels it too. "We shouldn't." His voice is barely audible.

"But we're going to."

When I reach him, he's trembling. His breath fans across my cheek, warm and human and real. I press my hand to his chest, and his heart is hammering beneath it.

"I'm not possessed," I say softly. "This is me."

He looks at me then. And whatever he sees in my face breaks his resolve.

He grabs me like he's starving.

Our mouths crash together, tongues tangling, teeth clashing. It's not gentle. It's not sweet. It's need.

We stumble backward, knocking into the camera tripod. It topples with a crash, but neither of us stops.

Nate lifts me onto the sheet-covered card table. My legs wrap around his waist. His hands push up my shirt, sliding over my ribs, my breasts, and I arch into him with a gasp.

Behind my eyes, Roman hums.

*That's it, Dove. Let him take you for me.*

Nate tears his mouth away from mine and freezes.

"You heard him," I whisper.

He nods. Just once.

Then he tugs my shirt up over my head and resumes kissing

me with ferocious energy. I slide my hands under his t-shirt and feel taut muscles. A hum escapes my mouth and presses into his. He returns it with a low moan. I break the kiss and yank his shirt over his head.

His fingers fumble with the button on my jeans and mine with his. It's clumsy, frantic, desperate. I need him like I've never needed anything. But I need Roman too for it to be complete.

Roman purrs inside me at that and I feel more of him fill me, like water pouring into a jar.

I get Nate's jeans down over his hips and he tears mine down my legs, tugging them off with my shoes and tossing them aside. His body drives into me and his mouth is back on mine in an instant. Hungry. Starving.

He pushes his cock into me with a groan that's half agony, half relief.

It's fast. It's furious. Our bodies moving in a rhythm neither of us sets. The small table beneath me slips across the floorboards, banging against the wall with each pounding thrust.

I moan my way rapidly towards a climax. My body coiling tight, ready to burst.

Roman is there with us, excitement pulsing from the energy that I recognise as not mine and not Nate's. I don't know if Nate can feel it like I can, but his enthusiasm is undeniable. His hands grasp my hips hard, his breath is hot and ragged against my mouth and neck as he flits between desperately kissing me and pulling back for air.

The sensor on the wall flashes in time with our thrusts—Roman's pulse echoing in the room, watching, feeding, joining.

I cry out, the sound strangled against Nate's shoulder. He clutches me tighter, like he wants to anchor me—but we're both already gone.

As I come, Roman's cold breath whispers across my neck.

*Good girl.*

Nate follows seconds later, shuddering against me, his face buried in my hair. The swell of him inside me sends an aftershock through my nerves and I whimper again.

Silence swells around us in the aftermath. The lights flicker once, then settle. The monitor blinks back to black.

We're alone again.

But not really.

We never were.

# CHAPTER SEVEN

We don't speak as we clean up the mess.

Words feel too fragile. Too human. And whatever passed between us moments ago wasn't just sex—it wasn't just us. It was more, and it still hangs in the air like a charge after lightning. Speaking would break it, and I don't know if I want it broken yet.

The tripod lies where it fell, splayed out awkwardly like a dead insect. One leg is bent at an unnatural angle, and the cord has pulled free, looping across the floor like a noose. The notepad I'd been using earlier is across the room, half beneath the table, pages torn loose and scattered like brittle leaves. A few are crumpled, as if something—or someone—stepped on them mid-thrust.

I crouch and begin collecting them slowly, the paper whispering under my fingers. I don't remember knocking it over. Don't remember dropping it. Truthfully, I don't remember much after I wrapped my legs around Nate and let go of the last tether to who I thought I was.

The room is warmer now. Not just the physical heat of sweat and skin and exertion, but something deeper. The kind of warmth that soaks into the walls. That stays. The air smells faintly of candle wax and sex, despite neither being lit.

It feels like the house is pleased. Like we did exactly what it wanted.

Nate finishes coiling the mic cord with the kind of mechanical precision he always uses when he doesn't want to feel something. He straightens with a tired grunt, and I catch a glimpse of him in my periphery—his t-shirt clings to his body, damp at the collar and stretched slightly at the hem from where I yanked it earlier. His knuckles are scraped. His mouth is red, kissed raw. His jaw tight, clenched like he's trying to hold something back.

I can't look at him for long. Not because I'm ashamed of what we did. But because I'm not sure which part of it I wanted more—Nate's body, Roman's presence, or the way they blurred together so seamlessly I lost the ability to care.

He hasn't said a word since we pulled apart and remembered we were two separate people again.

Three.

The thought comes unbidden. Unavoidable.

My skin prickles with the ghost of cold breath on my throat, as if Roman had leaned in to whisper something and changed his mind at the last second. He didn't say anything when it ended. No smug purr. No dark praise. He just... faded. Slipped out of me like smoke.

But he's still here.

Watching.

I can feel it.

I cross the room slowly, knees still weak, thighs still slick. My shirt is balled in the corner where I dropped it—torn from me, or maybe I tore it off myself. I don't remember. I pick it up and give it a half-hearted shake, then pull it over my head. The fabric is cold, slightly damp with sweat, and clings to the curve of my back in an almost accusatory way. A reminder.

My jeans are in a heap near the toppled tripod. I step into them stiffly, wincing as the rough denim scrapes against the inside of my thighs. The friction stings. Not just from the sex. From the weight of it all. I feel scraped raw, like I've been sanded down from the inside out.

My hands pause at the button, and for a moment I just stand there, breathing.

"We need a break," Nate says, voice low and hoarse like he's been screaming. He hasn't. Not with his mouth.

I nod. "Ten minutes."

He snorts. "Ten hours."

It's not quite a joke, but it's the closest either of us has come to one in hours. I huff a breath that might be a laugh. It hurts, a little, in my chest.

"Go nap, then," I say, not looking at him.

"I can't," he mutters. "If I sleep now, I'm not waking up 'til morning."

I don't tell him that part of me wants that—to have him gone for a little while, so I don't have to feel his eyes on me, kind and confused and quietly breaking. I also don't tell him that another part wants him to stay right there, tethered to me, because I don't trust what might happen if I'm left alone again.

"I'll go…" He gestures vaguely at the equipment case in the corner. "Check the cameras. See what survived."

He doesn't meet my eyes.

I nod again, but he's already moving, walking like his body still isn't entirely his own.

He brushes past me, and something in the way he moves makes my heart lurch. He doesn't touch me, but the absence feels like one. A gentle severing. I want to reach for him. Say something. Apologise. Explain. Something. But the words knot in my throat.

Because the truth is, I don't know what's mine and what was Roman's any more.

Instead, I let my feet carry me, aimless and slow, through the hall like a sleepwalker. The house feels different now—denser somehow. Thicker in the air. Every creak of the floorboards underfoot sounds deliberate, like the bones of the house are cracking just to listen to me move.

My body aches in quiet places. I should shower. I should sleep. But I don't. I feel like I've been branded. Like something permanent has been written into my skin and it's still cooling, still settling in.

I find myself standing outside the study, not sure when I decided to stop there. My hand hovers over the doorknob. A chill trickles over my arms—not the thrilling cold of Roman's touch, but something older. Deeper. The house remembering. I feel it watching. Waiting to see what I'll do next.

I enter anyway.

The light in the study is thin, filtered through dusty glass. It gives everything a hazy, unreal quality, like stepping into an old photograph. Dust lies thick over the furniture again, as if the events of last night had been erased—scrubbed out by time, like they never happened at all.

But they did.

The ache between my legs tells me so. The fading flush in my skin. The echo of Roman's voice still curling in my head like smoke.

The desk drawer is open.

I'm sure it was closed earlier. I remember sitting on the desk as Nate straightened the paintings.

I cross the room on quiet feet, each step sinking into silence. The drawer's yawning mouth offers its secret willingly this time—no struggle, no creak. As if it wants me to find what's inside.

Beneath a stack of yellowed sketch paper, something catches my eye.

A folded letter, sealed with a blood-dark wax stamp. The wax is cracked in places, like dried scabs. The impression in the centre is ornate. The curve of an R.

Roman.

My fingers hover.

I don't know if I'm ready for what it says. I'm not sure I want to hear his voice again in this way—so intimate, so deliberate. The sex, the possession, the memory-dreams—they all had a heat to them. A fevered immediacy.

This is different. This is something he meant for someone else. Or maybe for me all along. I break the seal with a snap that sounds louder than it should in the stillness. The paper unfolds stiffly in my hands. The handwriting is elegant. Sharp. Slanted. Familiar.

I lower myself into the old armchair by the window, the letter open in my hands, creased softly in the middle like it's been unfolded and folded again too many times.

I start to read.

*My Dove,*

*I dreamed of you again last night.*

I swallow. The words already feel familiar. Like I've read them before, or maybe just wanted to.

*You came to me in the parlour and laid yourself bare. You let me draw every curve, every secret. You looked at me like I was more than the man I am, and I believed it—if only for the length of a breath.*

My chest tightens. The handwriting is steady, assured. He meant every word.

*I remember the heat of your skin under my hands. The weight of your gaze as I knelt between your thighs. The taste of you—salt and silk and something only I was allowed to know.*

I shift in the chair, acutely aware of the stillness pressing in around me. Of how easily I could close my eyes and fall back into that dream. How badly I want to.

*I remember the moment you opened for me—not just your body, but your soul. You let me in. And I would stay there, if I could. Curled inside your heart like a secret no one else gets to hold.*

A shiver moves through me.

It could be a memory. It could be a lie. It could have been meant for someone else entirely. But the way he writes it... it feels like now. Like he's watching me read it.

*One day, you will return to me. In skin or spirit, I do not care. I will know you by the way you look at me. The way you let me in.*

That line. It sits heavy behind my ribs.

*I miss your breath on my neck. The catch in your voice when you say my name. The way you tremble, even when you think you're not afraid.*

I'm trembling now.

I fold the letter slowly, careful not to crease it further, and lay it in my lap. My fingers brush the wax seal, now broken. Something permanent cracked open.

I stare at the dust motes floating in the slanted light from the window. They look like snow. Or ash.

Was this meant for her?

Or did he know I would come?

The letter lies warm in my lap from where my hands have held it too long. My fingertips trace the edge of the paper, over and over, like maybe if I keep touching it, the truth will reveal itself. Who it's for. When it was written. Whether he meant it for me… or if I'm just wearing the ghost of someone else.

The silence in the study shifts—softens.

It's not physical. The air doesn't change. The light doesn't flicker. But I feel it like a hand on my cheek. A breath I didn't take.

*You came back to me.*

The voice is only in my head. Gentle. Low. Possessive in a way that doesn't demand, only claims.

I close my eyes and exhale through parted lips. I don't respond. I don't have to. He already knows.

The warmth vanishes as quickly as it came, leaving the letter heavier in my hands.

I fold it carefully back along its worn crease and slide it between two loose sketchbooks in the drawer. My fingers linger on the paper before I close the drawer again. I don't lock it. There's no point. Nothing in this house stays shut.

When I find Nate, he's in the parlour, crouched beside the camera tripod. It's upright again, though slightly askew, and he's fiddling with the mount as if he can fix more than just the hardware.

He glances up when I enter. His eyes are tired. Not angry, not cold—just tired. Like he's been holding something in for too long and it's starting to burn.

"Tripod's done for," he mutters. "We've got a spare, but the socket's warped."

I nod and lower myself onto the covered sofa across from him. The old springs squeak beneath me. My body is still sore in quiet, embarrassing ways.

He stands, wiping his hands on his jeans, and looks at me for a long time. I wonder if he can smell Roman on me. If he can see what I've been doing. What I've been feeling.

"Everything okay?" he asks, as if that's not the most ridiculous question in the world.

I nod again. Lie again. "Fine."

He doesn't call me on it.

We hang suspended there, two people in a house that wants to keep us. And somewhere in the shadows between us, Roman waits. Smiling.

A soft creak sounds from the hallway.

Both of us freeze.

It's slow. Deliberate. The sound of weight settling into old floorboards just beyond the threshold.

Not the house settling. Not pipes or age or wind.

Footsteps.

Measured.

Listening.

Watching.

I meet Nate's gaze, and for a heartbeat, neither of us breathes.

He reaches for the camera instinctively. I don't move.

The sensor light on the far wall flickers once.

Then goes dark.

# CHAPTER EIGHT

The footsteps stop as suddenly as they began. Nate and I remain frozen, barely breathing, eyes locked across the dim parlour. The silence is too complete. No groan of settling pipes. No creak of cooling wood. Just stillness. Finally, he moves—slowly rising to his feet, one hand clutching the camera, the other curling instinctively into a loose fist.

"You heard that, right?" he murmurs.

I nod, my throat too tight to speak.

He crosses to the door and peers into the hallway, shoulders tense, every muscle in his back coiled tight like he's waiting for something to leap out at him. I move to join him, steps muffled by the thick layer of dust clinging to the floorboards, each one leaving a print behind like a breadcrumb trail through someone else's memory.

The hall is empty. The landing above looms in shadow, though light still filters weakly through the high window above the stairs, catching on the dust in the air. It's midday, but the house absorbs sunlight like a secret—nothing shines here. The beams stretch long and dull across the warped floorboards, more suggestion than illumination.

But the air feels wrong. Not just cool. Disturbed. Like someone just exhaled over the whole house—a long, deliberate breath. Not Roman's. Something heavier. Less patient.

Nate flicks the camera on to record and pans it slowly up the staircase.

I expect to see Roman. Part of me wants to. To believe it was just him, watching. Wanting. Testing. But the energy that lingers here isn't his. Roman's presence is cold but seductive. Intimate. Possessive. This is something else. Heavy. Pressing. Spiteful.

My breath catches, and for a moment, I think I'm going to say it—I know this isn't Roman—but the words stick. Because saying it makes it real.

I force a shrug instead. "The house is old. That board on the landing drops every time the wind shifts."

Nate gives me a look.

"I'm just saying," I add quickly. "We had a rough night. Maybe we're hearing things that aren't there."

He doesn't argue. Doesn't agree either.

Instead, he steps forward and ascends the stairs, slow and careful.

I follow.

The landing is just as we left it. No objects moved. No cold spots. The broken banister piece still lies where it fell on the stairs.

But the house is listening.

I can feel it now. Not just Roman. Not even just one thing.

Many.

I blink the thought away. Focus. The mirror at the end of the landing reflects us back in strange, stretched angles. Nate keeps the camera steady. His steps make no sound, even though mine do.

"Anything feel off to you?" he asks without looking back.

My mouth is dry. "No. Not really."

Lie.

I brush a chill off my arm that didn't come from the air. It felt like fingertips. Brief, curious. Wrong.

The upstairs doors are all still shut. The study, the bedrooms, the shattered guest room. Everything looks untouched. But I know it isn't. Roman isn't the only one watching.

We check each room one by one, Nate pushing each door open ahead of me like we're entering a crime scene. Nothing has moved. Nothing is out of place. But that doesn't mean it's right.

When we reach the guest room—the one with the broken window and the hole in the floor—we pause on the threshold. The cold seeps out like breath from an open mouth. It crawls over my skin, light and sticky, like cobwebs that don't quite touch.

Nate steps inside. I stay in the doorway.

The curtains shift. Just a little.

Nate frowns and pans the camera slowly toward them. "No breeze."

"There's a window," I offer, but it sounds weak even to me. The window is broken, but the air outside is still.

He doesn't call me on it. Instead, he bends to examine the floor. The shards of glass remain undisturbed. The splintered boards gape the same as before. But something's changed. There's a trail through the dust. Barely perceptible. A faint drag like someone moved slowly across the floor, brushing their hand or gown or body through the layer of grime.

"Nate," I whisper, stepping in beside him now. "Did we check this room yesterday?"

"We looked in. We didn't enter."

"So who walked through it?"

He doesn't answer.

The camera beeps. Recording.

We return downstairs, the weight of silence hanging over us like wet cloth. Nate sets up the laptop on the table in the parlour —the scene of our passionate indiscretion—and loads the most recent audio files.

I sit cross-legged on the sofa, watching dust motes swirl in a shaft of light, feeling my skin tighten the longer we wait.

The file opens. The recording begins. First: silence. Room tone. The low hum of the camera. The faint shuffle of our boots. Then, in the gap between our voices—

A whisper.

It's soft. So soft I almost miss it. A word, maybe. Or a breath shaped like one. Nate rewinds. We listen again. Still faint, but clearer now.

*Get out.*

I press my hand to my chest.

Roman's voice is deep. Distinctive. Familiar. This... isn't his.

Nate pauses the playback.

"You heard that, right?" he asks, too evenly.

I nod, heart in my throat. But the lie is already forming.

"It's probably just interference. A feedback loop from the camera picking up our voices too early. Could even be background noise from the room."

He doesn't even look at me.

"Right," he says.

I don't blame him for not believing me. Because I don't believe me either.

The whisper on the recording lingers long after Nate shuts the laptop. The words—get out—echo in my head with too much clarity. Not Roman. I'm sure of it.

At least, I want to be.

Nate says nothing as he packs the equipment away again, movements clipped, jaw tight. I watch him from the sofa, arms wrapped around myself. I don't want to talk about what we heard. Not yet. I don't want to say out loud that there might be someone else here—something not Roman. Not when I'm only just starting to feel like I understand him.

Nate closes the laptop with a snap. "We should recheck the sensors upstairs," he says, not looking at me. "The landing one keeps dropping out."

I nod, following him out of the room, the house groaning faintly beneath our footsteps like it's listening again.

At the foot of the stairs, his hand brushes mine. Not deliberately—just enough to jolt something inside me. My pulse skips. My fingers twitch. I glance at him, and his eyes flick briefly to mine before dropping away again.

We're both thinking about it.

About before.

About him.

I shiver—not from cold, but from the slow, creeping awareness of being touched.

Roman's presence settles behind me like a second skin. No breath this time. No whisper. Just pressure—an invisible hand resting at the small of my back, guiding me up the stairs behind Nate.

By the time we reach the landing, my skin is flushed.

Nate bends to check the sensor box by the banister, crouched low, t-shirt stretching over the curve of his back. My eyes stray, unwillingly at first. Then with intent.

Roman's hand slides over my hip.

There's nothing there. No visible sign. But I feel it. Like the trace of a memory I didn't make.

My thighs press together.

Nate stands. Turns. Sees me standing on the landing half way to the master bedroom, eyes glazed, lips parted.

He crosses the space between us. Fast. Intentional.

"You feel him right now, don't you?" he asks, voice quiet but taut with heat.

I don't answer. Because yes. I do. I feel Roman's fingers at my throat. Nate's eyes on my mouth. The space between us charged so thick I could drown in it.

Nate's hand rises, brushing hair from my cheek. His knuckles graze my jaw. I sway into it without meaning to.

"I don't know what this is," he murmurs. "But I can't stop wanting it."

I exhale slowly, Roman's breath echoing mine, invisible but present.

"I don't want you to stop."

Nate leans in. Kisses me softly this time, like he's afraid of who might be watching. My lips part under his, and the kiss deepens. Roman presses against my back, cool and unyielding.

His chill coils low in my belly, stirring heat in its wake.

My fingers fist in Nate's hair. His hand cups the back of my neck. I'm pinned between them—man and ghost, past and present. One holding me. One haunting me.

Nate's hand slides under my shirt, over my ribs, up to the curve of my breast. I gasp against his mouth.

Roman hums approval inside my mind.

I'm right on the cusp of giving in to this, whatever this is, again. But that other presence lingers like a shadow. Tense. Tight. Threatening.

And that's when I stop.

Pull away.

Breathe.

"Not here," I whisper.

Nate's chest heaves with restraint. He nods, steps back.

We stand there, the three of us, in the quiet aftermath of almost. The mirror at the end of the landing catches our reflection—just two flesh and blood people. No one else. As if to remind me that for all the weight pressing in, for all the hands I feel... only Nate and I are really here.

We drift apart like smoke, each of us too aware of the other's breathing. Of our own.

Nate steps away first, rubbing the back of his neck like he's trying to shake something off. I press my palm flat to my chest to calm the flutter beneath it, but my hand lingers longer than it should.

I glance down the hall.

The mirror no longer reflects anything but a smear of light and shadow. The figures we saw—ourselves—are gone. Just blurred edges now, a smudged hint of motion. Like the mirror forgot what it was supposed to remember.

"I'll check the bedrooms again," Nate says, his voice too casual.

I nod and walk away, already retreating down the stairs, needing air, space, anything but this tension curling tighter around me with every breath.

I duck into the dining room, not even sure why. Maybe just because it's empty. It's one of the few places in the house that hasn't been used against us.

I lean against the edge of the long, dusty table and close my eyes.

*Get out.*

The voice from the recording resurfaces in my mind—not a whisper now, but a weight. A presence pressing at the back of my skull.

Something shifts behind me.

I spin.

Nothing.

But the dust has moved. A faint impression in the layer of grey atop the table—dragged fingers. Four of them. Light, uneven. Not mine. They curve at the end like claws.

I back up slowly, breath catching in my throat.

It's not Roman. I have to admit that now.

Because Roman touches me with reverence. With obsession. With need. This felt different. Like spite.

Nate's footsteps thud upstairs. The squeak of an old hinge. A creak of shifting weight.

And then—

A bang.

Not loud. Not violent. But sharp. Intentional. Coming from the kitchen.

My heart slams against my ribs.

I don't call out. I don't run.

I just listen.

And in the distance, behind the walls, I swear I hear a woman laugh.

The laugh fades into silence, but the echo of it vibrates in my bones.

I move toward the kitchen, pulled more than walking, feet barely whispering over the floorboards. The hallway narrows as I approach, and the shadows stretch longer, pooling in the corners like spilled ink.

The door is ajar. Just enough to see a sliver of tiled floor beyond.

I push it open.

The kitchen is a drab, hollow room, all faded linoleum and warped cabinetry. A single bare bulb dangles from the ceiling, swaying slightly like it's been disturbed. The wallpaper is peeling in wide strips, revealing flaking plaster beneath. It smells faintly of rust and rot and the metallic memory of something long since gone.

The light from the parlour doesn't reach this far. It feels like the room exists in its own pocket of shadow.

The sink is empty, but the basin is ringed with a line of greenish muck, like something once sat there too long and left behind the memory of rot. The tap drips steadily, staining the enamel below with faint rust trails that spider down toward the drain.

There's a coat hook by the door, the rusted kind with bent prongs. A stained apron still hangs from it, patterned with faded sunflowers. One of the pockets is torn. My breath stutters when I realise it's been recently tugged—one side hangs lower, the fabric stretched.

I step forward, slowly.

The air here is colder than the rest of the house. Not Roman's familiar chill, not the seductive creep of his presence. This is dead air. Hollow. Like a room that's been waiting a long time for someone to step back inside.

The laugh doesn't return.

But something else does.

A clink.

Metal on metal.

It comes from inside the old larder. A tall cupboard with a half-broken handle and a warped door that leans slightly open. I inch toward it, pulse thudding in my ears.

Another clink. Then silence.

I reach out and touch the door. It swings inward with a soft groan. A wave of air rolls out—damp and sour, like mould clinging to forgotten tins and the long-decayed ghosts of food.

Then—

A flash of white at the edge of my vision. A sudden presence right behind me.

I spin.

No one's there.

But the apron swings slightly on its hook, like it's just been passed through.

"Rae?"

I flinch.

Nate stands in the doorway, eyes wide, scanning the room. "What's wrong? What happened?"

I open my mouth.

Then close it.

Because I don't know how to explain what I didn't see.

Just what I felt.

# CHAPTER NINE

We spend the afternoon with the doors and windows open wide.

The air in the house has been too still for too long—thick with memory, dust, and things that don't want to move on. Getting the air flowing is the first step in any proper clearing. That, and sweeping.

I find an old broom in the kitchen, its handle dry and splintering, the bristles stiff and warped from neglect. It's barely functional, but it's better than nothing. I sweep in long, methodical strokes—front to back, always toward the door, like I'm coaxing something unseen out of the corners. Every pass sends up clouds of dust and shivers of unease.

Nate props the front and back doors open, checks the windows upstairs. Light and air spill in reluctantly, like the house doesn't appreciate the intrusion. The beams of sunlight stretch long and pale through the dusty air, touching surfaces that haven't been exposed in years.

We say very little as we work.

There's something calming about the rhythm. Dust into piles. Energy into motion. The house resists at first—floorboards creak with annoyance, a door slams upstairs despite the wedge. But gradually, the pressure lifts. Not entirely. Just enough to breathe.

I work my way through the hall, then the parlour, then into the study where the paintings once stood like silent witnesses. They're now back as we found them—wrapped in sheets and tucked in a corner, out of sight but not forgotten.

By the time the sun dips lower, the worst of the dust is gone. The windows let in a breeze. The air smells faintly of old wood and cracked plaster, but it's better than it was. Cleaner. Lighter.

Almost liveable.

I sit for a moment at the base of the stairs, hand still resting on the broom handle. My legs ache. My shoulders are tight. But something in me feels steadier. Like I've carved out a pocket of peace in the chaos.

Even if it won't last.

By late evening, the air has changed. It's still heavy in places, still clings to the walls like damp wallpaper, but it moves now. Breathes. And that's something. I haven't felt another presence in all the time I've been cleaning. Nate and I felt very much alone here, as if the restless spirits were hiding from the broom.

In the parlour, lit only by our glaring white light running on our generator, I finally turn my attention to the furniture—each piece long buried beneath dust sheets that hang like ghost-shrouds.

I start with the largest shape in the corner, tugging the sheet free with slow, careful hands. Dust billows into the air, catching the fading sunlight in soft gold clouds.

A grand old piano stands beneath. The surface is dull with grime, the keys yellowed and cracked, but it has weight. Presence.

A dark and elegant thing, silent now but still regal in the way old things are when they've been respected.

Next, I move to the chaise lounge.

I already know what it is. What it was. My hands tremble a little as I peel back the cloth.

It's even more beautiful than I expected. The upholstery is faded—a delicate blush that's dulled to the colour of old roses—but the shape is unmistakable. Curved, inviting. The silk is fraying in places, the wood frame nicked and softened by time. But I see it, the way it used to be. The way it looked in the paintings. The way she looked when she reclined there, half-dressed, smiling like she knew every secret I didn't.

I run my fingertips lightly over the fabric. The silk still has that whispery texture, cool under my skin. Almost like a kiss.

She sat here. Again and again. Posed. Watched. Loved?

Or… studied. Obsessed over. Captured.

I trail my hand down the armrest, then curl into the seat like I'm slipping into someone else's place. My head rests against the back cushion. My eyes drift closed.

Just for a moment.

The air shifts.

The light bends.

And the house forgets what century it's in.

I open my eyes to firelight.

Not the harsh white glare of the portable lamp, but the soft flicker of an open hearth casting gold across polished wood and silk.

The parlour is transformed.

The dust is gone. The air is warm and heavy with beeswax, smoke, and something floral—lavender or rose water, maybe. The piano gleams. Candles flicker in silver sconces. The chaise beneath me is whole, its silk vibrant and unblemished. It cradles my body like it remembers me.

Except I'm not me.

My clothes are gone. In their place: a corseted bodice, sheer chemise, and a long, gathered skirt I don't remember putting on. I raise a trembling hand to my chest. Even my nails are manicured. Painted. Pale rose pink.

I sit up slowly.

The house is quiet, but not empty. There's a hum in the walls. A tension in the air, like anticipation curled into every shadow.

The fire cracks.

I glance toward the door just as it opens.

Roman enters.

Not his voice in my head, not his chill coiling down my spine, but him—flesh and blood, as he must have looked in life. Tall. Impeccably dressed in dark trousers and a linen shirt, sleeves rolled to his elbows. Paint smudges on his fingers. He smells of oil and turpentine, smoke and skin.

His eyes find me instantly.

"Ah," he says, smiling slowly. "You're here."

I try to speak, but no words come. My lips part. Nothing escapes.

Roman crosses to me in three long steps, kneels beside the chaise, and takes my hand like it's the most natural thing in the world.

"You always look your best in firelight," he murmurs, thumb stroking over my knuckles. "So soft. So alive."

I shiver.

His hand slides up my arm, then down to the curve of my waist, anchoring me there.

"You remember this, don't you?" he whispers. "You asked me to show you. And I always keep my promises."

I was confused already but now… is he talking to me, or her? Is this a memory or a dream?

He leans in. His breath is warm on my face. His cheeks are flushed. His dark eyes are penetrating and I surrender to him. His kiss is deep, warm, intoxicating. Utterly real.

Whether I'm myself or his muse, I no longer care. I give in to this. I thread my manicured fingers through the curls of his hair. He tastes of tobacco but he smells of paint. Where his smudged fingers squeeze my breasts, traces of the dark red paint transfer to the silk of my dress and the curve of bare skin.

He's hitching up my skirts now, his hands searching for *me*. I'm untucking his shirt, my hands scrambling for skin.

The heat between us rivals the heat of the fire crackling behind him in the grate.

I gasp for breath between frantic kisses.

His fingers find my warm centre among all that fabric and everything slows. He slides one finger slowly into me and our mouths part, wide and gasping but not quite touching. Our eyes are locked onto one another. In this moment I'm certain that I'm myself and he is with me. This is no memory.

And then—something shifts.

A crack in the candlelight. A rift in the air. A loud snap from the fire.

I pull back. His finger slides swiftly out of me and he rocks back on his heels.

Roman's expression twists. Not in anger. In confusion.

The fire gutters. Goes out. Plunging the room into near darkness with just a few candles flickering feebly against a strong breeze.

A sharp scent fills the air—metallic. Wet.

I blink and the chaise beneath me is damp. Sticky. I look down.

Blood.

Soaking into the silk like it's always been there.

Roman rises to his feet, mouth opening like he's about to speak—but behind him, the shadows move.

She steps out of them. The woman from the paintings. Naked. Bloodied. Her throat slit deep and glistening. Her hair hangs in sodden curls. Her mouth opens, a scream stretching her features into something unrecognisable. She's looking at me.

Roman shouts something I don't understand. His voice warps. Fades.

The woman lunges. Her fingers claw into my arms and pull.

The scream tears through me. Not hers—mine. But it never leaves my throat.

The woman's blood-slick hands clamp down on my arms, yanking, dragging, pulling me out of myself. Her mouth stretches impossibly wide. No sound. Just void. Darkness flooding in—

I jolt awake with a gasp so violent my back arches off the chaise.

Air. I can't find it.

My hands claw at my throat. My chest is convulsing, lungs burning, choking on something that isn't there.

"Rae—Jesus, Rae—!"

Nate.

His voice cuts through the chaos like a blade. He's there. Kneeling beside me, hands on my shoulders, trying to steady me as I thrash.

"Breathe—come on—look at me. Look at me!"

My eyes find his. Blue. Real. Present.

I suck in a ragged breath that turns into a sob.

He pulls me into a sitting position, cradles my head to his shoulder, one hand cupping the back of my neck like he's afraid I'll slip away again.

"You were making these awful noises," he murmurs. "Like—like you couldn't breathe. I didn't know what to do."

"I couldn't," I whisper. My throat feels raw. "She was... she grabbed me."

He pulls back just enough to see my face. "Who?"

I shake my head, still gasping. "The woman. From the paintings."

His expression darkens. "You saw her?"

"She was in the dream. At first it was just Roman. But she came... and she pulled me."

I look down. My arms ache. I lift my sleeves. Angry red scratches rake down my forearms, not bleeding, but vivid.

Nate's jaw clenches.

"Okay," he says. Voice tight. Controlled. "Okay, we need to talk about this. Because that's not just a dream. And this isn't just Roman any more."

I nod slowly, still trembling.

He sits back on his heels, raking a hand through his hair. "Whoever—or whatever—she is, she doesn't want you here. That wasn't a warning. That was an attack."

"She was trying to drag me under," I whisper. "Like she wanted to... take me. Replace me."

Nate looks at me, his face drawn. "You said you were with Roman, and then she came. So what—was it a memory? A vision? Possession?"

"I don't know." I press the heel of my hand to my chest, trying to steady my breath. "It felt real. Not just a scene. Not something he showed me. Like I was there. Living it."

"And then she hijacked it."

"Yeah."

We sit in silence for a long moment.

The parlour feels darker now, despite the light spilling from the portable light by the piano.

"So what does that mean for us?" Nate finally asks. "If there's another spirit in this house—and she's strong enough to hurt you..."

He trails off.

But I hear the real question.

What happens if this stops being about sex and memory and ghosts who want to touch us?

What happens if this turns into a fight we're not ready for?

"We have to do our job," I say, ready to commit to it. Even if it means losing Roman. "We have to clear the house."

# CHAPTER TEN

Nate busies himself with checking all of the equipment, making sure the cameras are covering all angles of the parlour and hall. I pace in front of the boarded up fireplace and try to ready myself for what has to be done.

My skin prickles and the deep cold of the house gets into my bones.

"Ready?" Nate asks, when all of his technical work is complete.

I nod and flex my fingers.

Nate positions himself behind one of the cameras, near his laptop, headphones over his ears.

I take a deep breath and close my eyes.

"Roman? Are you here?"

I'm met with silence.

I remove my jumper, even though it's freezing. I want to give him skin to touch, as I know that's how he communicates. My t-shirt neck hangs loose, one shoulder exposed.

"Roman. I'd like you to talk to me."

Silky cold tendrils whisper over my skin. He presses against my back, his hands caressing my throat and then raking down my arms, over the scratches left by the other spirit.

*She hurt you.*

His voice purrs, concern laced over his desire for me.

"She did. Roman? Who is she?"

*A problem.*

"Yes. I see that. Is she here now?"

Silence.

I peek a look at Nate, who is frowning down at his laptop screen, his face lit with its ghostly glow.

A thump breaks the silence and my gaze darts to the ceiling over my head. Another thump.

Nate looks up too.

"It's coming from the master bedroom," he says.

"Uh-huh." I reply, my gaze fixed on the ceiling. Cobwebs still cling to the cracked plaster, shining in the glare of our bright lamp.

*That is her.*

"Who is she, Roman?"

*You know, my Dove. You've seen her portraits.*

"Yes, but I don't even know her name. Can you tell me?"

His cold hands roam over my exposed skin. His need to be with me is potent. The scent of sulphur creeps into the room.

*Thump. Thump. Thump.*

Nate swiftly unclips the camera from the tripod and dashes from the room. His footsteps bound up the stairs. I stand frozen, held in place by Roman's hands on my throat and waist.

"Rae!" Nate calls.

I tear free of Roman's grasp and run from the room. I take the stairs two at a time as that incessant thumping continues, accompanying my footsteps on the wooden floor. I fly around the corner at the top of the stairs and join Nate in the doorway of the master bedroom.

The huge bed is rising and dropping in a steady rhythm.

*Come away from there.* Roman insists, his icy touch returning to my bare arm.

My gaze drifts from the thumping bed to the dark stain on the wooden floor, illuminated by the hint of moonlight shining in through the window.

"What the—?" Nate pans the camera around the room, taking in the bed's movement.

*Please.* Roman's pull on me intensifies and my arm actually moves away from my body as if he's really tugging on it. I look into the space beside me and catch a glimpse of my reflection in the mirror. A gentle flare of light hovers beside me. I gently touch Nate's arm and he swivels towards me. I point towards the mirror and he directs the camera at it.

*Crack.*

I startle as a jagged black line appears in the glass. Roman's icy touch vanishes and a roar fills the house. The scream of rage. It isn't Roman.

A rush of energy sweeps from the mirror towards me and my breath catches. Nate grabs my arm and drags me into the now silent bedroom. He kicks the door closed and something impacts the other side of it with a heavy thud and the hinges rattle.

"Fuck." I gasp, trying to catch my breath.

"You okay?" Nate asks, the camera hanging at his side in one hand as his other hand cups my cheek.

"Yeah. I'm all right." I scan the room. We're alone. The bed is still. The air is frigid. But the scent of death clings to the air and every surface in this room. My gaze lingers on that dark stain. Something awful happened here.

Nate moves away from me and places the camera on the mantle piece, pointing out into the room. He returns to my side and wraps his arms around me.

"Did you get her name?" His breath flutters over my hair.

I grasp his back, my arms locked tight around him.

"Not yet. Nate, she's so angry."

"I got that." He holds me even tighter and warmth spreads though my body from his. "I've got you. Nothing can happen to you."

I tilt my head up without loosening my grip on him. My lips graze his jaw, lightly at first, but then with more intention. I never knew how much I needed him before, how he grounds me. Fear still flutters through my body, but in Nate's arms, nothing bad can touch me.

Our lips meet and a soft kiss brushes between them.

The fear ebbs from my body and I sink into his embrace.

I shouldn't want this. Not here. Not now. But my body craves his touch and the safety of intimacy with him. He's peeling off my clothes and there's nothing I can do to resist this. I unfasten his jeans and my hand reaches past the denim to grasp his erection.

His gasp breaks our kiss. We hurriedly shed our clothes fully and he pushes me up against the wardrobe. He pins my wrists above my head with one hand, while the other grasps my thigh and hitches it up over his hip. He drives into me with one swift thrust and my back arches.

"Yes!" I cry out.

Roman isn't here and part of me feels like I'm betraying him. But I need Nate so badly, his grounding energy, his warmth.

Nate's thrusts are slow and deep. His breath is hot and ragged on my cheek. He moans with each deliberate stroke.

"Fuck, Rae. You feel incredible right now."

"You too. Oh God. I need you. Give me more."

He releases my wrists and scoops up my other leg, pinning me to the wardrobe door. He thrusts harder. Faster. My hands cling to his shoulders.

My climax rushes upon me suddenly, almost from nowhere and I cry out against his cheek. My pussy clenches around his cock and he moans, his lips against my collar bone now.

The unmistakable feeling of being watched creeps upon me as I come down from my orgasm, but it feels alien. Not Roman. The aftershock of my climax fizzles out with the creeping sensation.

But Nate's thrusts are unrelenting, even as dread replaces desire for me.

"Fuck," he whimpers. His release follows swiftly. He fills me and slows his thrusts. "Rae."

I cling to him, trying to stay present with him. This is real. This is physical. It matters.

Slowly, he pulls out of me and lowers my feet to the floor. His cum trickles out of me but we just stand there naked and holding each other.

She's still there. I feel her distinctly now. She's watching us and seething. But she doesn't act and I wonder if she only wants to keep me away from Roman.

Roman. I pull away from Nate, suddenly aware of Roman on the other side of the wall behind me. I feel him, his anger, his resentment.

"Roman can't come in here." I press my fingers to my lips, immediately sorry that another man's name is the first thing I utter after such intense sex with Nate.

Nate doesn't flinch. He locks his shrewd and honest eyes upon me and gently touches my shoulders.

"Why not?"

"This is her domain." I look past him to the fireplace and a trace of light hovers there, at the foot of the bed.

"She's here now, isn't she?"

I nod slowly. Nate turns and looks around the room, still holding my shoulders. He returns his gaze to me and releases my shoulders. "Let's get out of here."

I nod mutely. We gather our clothes and quickly pull on the essentials. Nate grabs the camera from the mantle, which, I realise, will have recorded our tryst in all its glory. I carry my jeans and boots and we hastily leave the room and head along the landing.

Roman is instantly around me, covering me with his cool touch. His hands roam all over my body and I just stand there on the landing, shivering as he explores my body.

Nate watches, his mouth slightly agog. As if he can see something.

*Are you unharmed?*

"I'm fine."

Roman's icy touch runs over my inner thighs, where Nate's sticky release clings to my skin.

Nate's on me then, wrapping his arms around me and the three of us hold each other. Relief washes through me. Not jealousy. Not anger. Not even desire. Just a tender sense of home. The three of us. Together.

*I cannot protect you in there.*

"Roman," I whisper.

Nate's grip tightens slightly.

"Who is she?" I ask.

*Adeline. The love of my life. And the cause of my death.*

"Oh." I pull out of Nate's arms, a frown etched on my brow. "He says her name is Adeline and that she caused his death." I relay to Nate. He steps back. His jeans are on but unfastened and his t-shirt is clutched in the same hand as the camera. He tilts his head and examines me.

"Interesting."

*You mustn't go in there.*

"We have to. We have to get close to her to help her to move on. Roman, she can't stay here."

"There's a sense of her in the parlour too," Nate says, his head still thoughtfully tilted.

"True. Maybe we can connect with her there."

*Yes, Roman says, his voice soft but eager. The parlour is where she lived. The bedroom is where she died.*

That revelation settles in the pit of my stomach like a heavy stone. My eyes widen and I'm about to relay this to Nate when he straightens his head with resolve.

"So," Nate says before I can speak. "How do we get rid of her?"

Nate's body bends abruptly at the naval and he is yanked away from me. An expression of wide-eyed shock clings to his face as he tumbles backwards through the hole in the banister.

"Nate!" I lurch forwards, trying to grab hold of him, but he falls away from me and lands with a heavy thud on the stairs below. "Nate!"

# CHAPTER ELEVEN

The sound of Nate's body hitting the stairs echoes through the house like a gunshot. Several lighter thumps follow.

My scream tears itself loose without permission. I fly down the landing, skidding barefoot across the warped floorboards. Roman's hands claw at my arms, trying to stop me, but I tear through him like fog.

"Nate!"

He's crumpled on the stairs, half on his back, half twisted, one leg tucked under him at an angle that looks wrong. His eyes are wide and glassy, lips parted around shallow, stuttering breaths.

I jump over him and drop to my knees on the step below him. The camera he'd been holding lies a few steps lower, the flip-out screen broken off. My attention leaps back to Nate's crumpled form.

"Oh my God—Nate—"

His mouth twitches.

"I'm okay," he lies. "I just—need a sec."

"You're not okay."

I press my hands to his chest, his arms, his ribs. No blood.

No obvious breaks. But there's bruising already blooming along one side of his torso, and the angle of his left foot turns my stomach.

"You need a hospital."

"No." He grabs my wrist, hard. "No way."

"Your ankle—"

"I'll strap it." He grits his teeth and winces as he shifts. "We can't leave now. We're too close."

He's pale. Sweating. But stubborn as hell.

Above me, the air chills.

Roman.

*You see now. I warned you. She is not like me.*

"I know," I whisper. "But you didn't stop her."

*I tried.*

I believe him. And I don't. My trust is cracking in all directions.

Nate tries to sit up and groans.

"Stop," I say, bracing him gently. "Just wait. I'll get your bag."

I rush down to the parlour. Everything looks wrong now. Dim. Tilted. The remaining camera still points at the empty space where I begged for Roman. Where I thought we could control this.

I tear through Nate's things until I find the first aid kit. When I return, he's breathing through his nose in short, practised bursts, sweat glistening along his temple.

"You're not fine," I mutter.

"No," he admits. "But I'm not dead."

Not yet.

I kneel at Nate's feet, unzipping the kit with shaking hands. Inside is a scattering of bandages, gauze, tape, antiseptic wipes—a mix of essentials and just-in-case items. Nothing that'll fix a twisted ankle, but enough to make do.

"Let me see."

He winces as I ease his boot off, peeling the sock away carefully. His ankle is already swelling, the skin taut and flushed. I press gently along the bone, testing.

He hisses through his teeth. "Still lucky it's not broken."

"Not so lucky that she threw you down a flight of stairs."

I reach for a roll of gauze and a pair of scissors. "This'll have to work for now."

I wind the gauze tight, layer after layer, then use medical tape to hold it in place. Not a brace. But enough to compress and protect.

"Stay off it," I murmur.

"Noted."

He props himself up on one elbow and watches me as I adjust the last of the tape. When my fingers brush the inside of his calf, he tenses—not from pain. From something else.

"You should be in a hospital," I say again.

"And leave you alone with her?"

I glance up. "I'm fine."

He gives me a look. "You're not. And neither am I. But we're all we've got right now."

I sit back on my heels. The stairs creak beneath us. Roman's chill still lingers nearby, quiet now. Almost… ashamed.

"Let's just get through tonight," I say. "We'll pack up in the morning."

Nate shakes his head slowly. "We're not leaving."

"You can't even walk properly."

"I'll crawl if I have to."

"Nate—"

"No." He grips my hand before I can pull away. His voice softens. "We came here to help. You don't walk away when something starts fighting back. That's when you dig in."

I blink at him, surprised by the conviction in his voice.

His thumb brushes over the scratches on my forearm. "She's scared of us. That's why she hit so hard."

I don't answer. I just let him hold my hand. The quiet settles again. A truce. For now.

Nate leans into me as I help him down the stairs, one arm draped over my shoulders. His weight is heavy but manageable, and the heat of his body pressed against mine settles something deep inside me. He's hurting, but he won't stop. And neither will I.

The parlour feels different now.

Less like a haunted room, more like a place we've claimed—even if only for the night. The chaise and the sofa sit bare under the dull glare of our portable lamp, the dust mostly cleared, the furniture worn but strangely comforting.

I lower Nate carefully onto the sofa. He sinks back with a hiss through his teeth, then exhales slowly.

"You should rest," I say, already grabbing a second blanket from the gear pile.

He laughs softly. "I'm not sleeping. Not after that."

"Okay. But you can rest without sleeping." I drape the blanket over him and help him to lie back, propping his injured ankle up on the arm of the sofa.

I return to the stairs. There's a chill, but the house is dormant, resting. It must have cost Adeline a great deal of power to push Nate like that. She'll be weak now. I scoop up the camera and examine the damage. It powers on with a touch. It's just the screen that's damaged.

I return to the parlour and shut the door, sealing us into the room that was once the source of life, joy and passion in this house.

"How bad is it?" Nate asks, his voice heavy with exhaustion.

"It still works." I pop out the SD card and plug it into the laptop, which I carry over to the sofa and place in my lap as I perch on the end beside Nate's head. I open the recording and skim through the footage Nate took. First of me by the fireplace in this very room, then his flight up the stairs. The thumping bed. Then the mirror. I swallow, discomfort and curiosity mingling.

I slow the footage down at the point where we start to undress each other. Nate stirs beside me and his hand slithers around my waist. His thumb caresses my side as we both watch the footage.

Roman is with us too. His icy touch rests over Nate's hand, echoing his movements.

We all watch Nate and I up against the wardrobe. Heat builds beneath my skin and between my thighs.

I turn it off once we see Nate pull out of me. I don't want to watch any further. I want to feel that heat again.

I set the laptop down and move myself to lie up against Nate, both of us stretched along the too-narrow seat.

For a while, we just lie in silence, listening to the low creaks of the house shifting, the soft hum of the lamp, the occasional crack of something cooling in the kitchen. There's no rush. Not right now. Just breath. Just being.

Then Nate speaks, voice low.

"I feel him, you know."

I look at him.

"Roman," he clarifies. "When I'm near you. When I touch you."

I don't respond. I want him to keep going.

"It's like he brushes up against me. Not invasive. Not angry. Just... there. Waiting." He runs a hand down his face. "And it should creep me out. It should make me jealous. But it doesn't."

My breath hitches.

He holds me close against his body, one hand brushing my thigh under the blanket.

"It turns me on," he says simply.

I swallow hard.

"Me too."

Roman's chill stirs the air around us, coiling in slow, silken loops. I feel him settle at my back, his presence neither urgent nor dominant—inviting. Waiting to be wanted.

And I do.

I press my lips against Nate's, kissing him, slow and soft. This time it's not frantic or frightened. It's grounded. Intentional. His lips part against mine and our hands begin to explore, each movement weighted with trust.

Roman wraps around me like a cloak.

His touch at my throat. His voice in my mind.

*Let me have you. Both of you.*

Nate pulls back just enough to look into my eyes. "Do you want this?"

I nod. "I want both of you."

Nate rolls me onto my back and carefully inches down my body, laying soft kisses on my chest, my stomach. His hands push my t-shirt up, exposing my belly.

Roman's cool touch explores my naked skin. He brushes over my mouth, spilling his icy essence into my parted lips.

I gasp just as Nate tugs my underwear down over my hips. He shuffles backwards along the sofa, wincing slightly with the movement of his injured ankle. But he doesn't relent.

Warmth from Nate covers my legs, his hot breath on my thighs. While Roman's fingers are all ice and intent, slipping over me with a patience that burns.

I give myself to both men.

Nate's tongue circles my clit, his warm fingers slip inside me.

Roman fills my mouth and presses against my breasts. I can imagine him, alive and hot with desire, straddling my chest, his cock in my mouth.

A moan rushes out of me and a ripple follows down my body and through the air.

The three of us writhe together in that sinful room, just as people did a hundred years ago.

The climax that fills my body is deep, raw and unyielding. It consumes me, body and soul. I float somewhere just outside my body, feeling everything and seeing everything. I see Roman now, a soft, pale shape of a man. He rides my face while reaching back and pressing a hand against Nate's back in a gesture of claiming.

Nate moans, his voice vibrating deliciously through my core.

The more I come, the more solid Roman becomes. And Nate isn't going to let me stop exploding over and over again.

I'm pressed against the silk sofa, lost to pleasure.

I'm barely aware of Nate moving up my body. I'm too far gone to really feel it when he eases his cock into me. Roman is all over me now. My body shivers with the cold.

But when Nate's heat cools inside me, I feel that and so does Nate. Our eyes lock onto each other, our breathing soft and fast.

"He's inside us," Nate whispers.

I nod and whimper.

"We're both inside you. Fuck." His mouth crashes down on mine.

Both of them move in me and it's exquisite. Rapturous.

The orgasm that bursts from my body is shattering. I know in that moment that I'll be forever changed by this. We have become one, the three of us.

Nate groans in my mouth as his cock swells inside me.

Roman sighs and the power he exudes makes his utterance audible, not just inside my head. It echoes off the walls. His climax makes the piano strings hum.

The three of us come together in one spectacular union. The powerless chandelier hanging from the ceiling begins to glow, flickering to life.

My body freezes and my gaze locks onto the light. Nate breaks our kiss and looks up.

The chandelier shakes, tinkling softly, and the light grows brighter.

"Roman? Is that you?"

*No, my Dove. It is not.*

# CHAPTER TWELVE

Nate pulls out of me and lurches backwards, his gaze still locked on the shaking light fitting.

I'm naked, raw, reeling from my epic climax, and fear judders in my heart.

Nate gets shakily to his feet, clutching the end of the sofa and keeping his weight of his hurt ankle. I look frantically from him, to the ceiling, to my discarded clothes. Conflicted. Desperate.

The solidity Roman found during sex is gone, there's nothing more than the feeling of his presence now and he's as afraid as I am.

The chandelier quivers and flickers one last time before falling still and dark.

"She really didn't like us doing that." Nate's voice is little more than a croak. He releases a shaking laugh.

*She has spent all her energy now.*

"What does that mean?" Nate asks. I look at him, frowning. He looks back at me, equally confused.

"Can you hear Roman's voice?"

"I think so. I heard that, at least."

"Oh good," Roman purrs. "That will make this so much easier."

"Fuck." Nate staggers backwards, wincing and limping all at once. His wet cock hangs between his thighs and I press my lips together to keep the hysterical laugh bubbling up inside me from leaking out.

"I think we're safe. For now." I manage to say. "Let's get dressed though, in case that changes."

I quickly clean myself up and get dressed before helping Nate back into his jeans. I fetch him a clean shirt from his bag. I drape it over his shoulders, trying not to wince as he threads his bruised arm into the sleeve. He lets out a sharp breath, then slumps down on the sofa with a groan, one hand pressed to his ribs, the other running through his hair.

"Okay," he murmurs. "That was a lot."

"Yeah," I agree, sinking down beside him, still pulling my hair back into some semblance of order. "Sex magic, ghost ménage, poltergeist tantrum. Just a regular Thursday night."

Nate lets out a low, breathless laugh. "It really shouldn't be funny, but I think I'm too tired to process anything else."

I hand him the blanket, and he pulls it over both of us as I settle beside him. The sofa is too small for two people, but we make it work—limbs tangled, heads close, warmth seeping between us where the house still breathes cold through the walls.

Roman curls around us like smoke.

His touch is soft now, feather-light. A cool hand at the back of my neck. A ghost of pressure where Nate's ribs are bruised.

"Rest, my Dove."

For the first time in days, I feel like I can.

Nate yawns and lets his head fall against mine. "Think we'll actually sleep?"

"We can try."

The house creaks overhead. Just wood settling. Just night stretching itself long.

Adeline is silent.

Roman hums somewhere between us, low and protective.

We sleep.

Light filters through the dusty windows in thin golden ribbons. I wake with my head on Nate's shoulder and his arm curled tight around my waist. Roman's presence hovers nearby—quiet, thoughtful. He didn't leave us in the night.

Nate stirs beside me, groaning as he tries to shift.

"Still here," he mutters. "Still broken."

I smile, then wince as I sit up.

"We lived," I say.

"Did more than that."

We spend a few minutes moving slowly—stretching, freshening up, re-wrapping Nate's ankle. The house feels lighter, like it's holding its breath. But we both know Adeline isn't gone. Just dormant.

"I think we have to deal with her today," I say as I press a fresh piece of tape over Nate's wrap.

"Yeah," he agrees. "We pushed her last night. She's not going to lie low for long."

"She's tethered to this house," I say. "But she's also tethered to Roman. That's what we need to understand."

Nate looks up at me, thoughtful. "You think it's unfinished business?"

"More than that. She's not just haunting the place. She's guarding it. Guarding him. Or maybe what happened between them."

I glance at the ceiling, towards the upstairs study, where Roman's paintings are still wrapped, tucked in the corner like bodies under sheets.

"We need the truth," I say softly. "What really happened. And how to let her go... without losing him."

Nate shifts, adjusting the weight off his ankle and leaning forward to rest his arm on his stronger knee. He's quiet for a beat. Then he says it—low, sure, and without hesitation.

"I want to keep him too."

I look at him, startled—but only a little. I shouldn't be surprised any more.

He meets my eyes. "Roman's part of this now. Of us. I don't know how it works, but I'm not ready to lose him either."

The air changes around us. Cooler. Steadier. Roman draws closer—no chill, no pressure—just presence.

"Thank you, Nate."

Nate flinches, but doesn't pull away.

"Still getting used to that," he mutters.

"Me too," I whisper, but warmth flutters in my chest.

Roman doesn't say anything more. He doesn't have to.

I get up slowly, stretching out the stiffness in my limbs. The ache of the night lingers, but it's a good ache. We're tired, sore, half broken—but alive. And now we know what we're fighting for.

"Let's start in the study," I say. "We need answers. And I think he's ready to give them."

Nate grabs the laptop and follows, limping but determined.

I help him up the stairs, taking it as slowly as he needs us to. We step into the study, the dust beginning to settle again. The wrapped paintings wait in the corner, still and silent.

I stand beside the stack, knowing which one is on top—the portrait of Adeline naked in the chaise. My fingers tremble slightly as I reach for the sheet.

"I think she was the last," I murmur. "But not the only one."

"Lover?"

"Muse."

I tug the cloth away.

Adeline's painted gaze meets mine. Still, cold, commanding.

"She's not going to go easy," Nate says, voice low.

"No," I whisper. "But we're not asking."

The painting stares back at me, her gaze heavy with secrets. Nate sets the laptop down on the desk, out of the way. I drag each of the paintings out to their own spot, leaning against the bookcases, like we did the first time. The study is quiet but watchful, like the walls remember more than they want to say.

The last painting is the largest—the canvas torn down the middle.

It's the orgy scene.

More decadent and detailed than I remembered. The brushwork is exquisite, fevered. Bodies intertwined, mouths open, hands gripping. The woman—Adeline—is at the centre. Reclined. Naked. Worshipped. Her eyes—Roman painted her looking directly at the viewer, but the expression isn't pleasure.

It's something sharper.

Something final.

A shudder ripples through me. Nate makes a small grunt of pain behind me and I turn to face him. He's leaning against the desk, looking at something on his computer screen, and rubbing a hand over his bruised ribs.

"Are you all right?" I move over to him and gently touch where he's clutching.

"Fine. I could use some stronger painkillers than what we have downstairs."

"I bet. I still think you should get medical help."

"No. I'm fine."

He isn't going to take my advice, so I keep it to myself. I turn my attention to the grand desk.

The drawers stick a little as I tug them open—most are filled with brittle paper, old receipts, yellowed sheet music, forgotten ink pots. But in the very back of the top drawer, tucked beneath a false panel that creaks under my fingers, I find something else.

A journal.

Bound in cracked leather, the cover soft with age and use. The pages are dense with ink—tight, slanted handwriting, neat in some places and erratic in others. Some entries are long and flowing. Others are little more than confessions scrawled in the margins.

I ease myself onto the desk, cross my legs and open the journal in my lap.

Nate leans close, silent.

The entries bleed with obsession. Pages filled with longing, lust, artistic hunger. Roman's voice unfurls across every line—intimate and terrifying.

*She was never just a muse. She wanted to be a mirror. To reflect me. Contain me. And I let her.*

*I painted her again today, though her smile has gone brittle. She watches the other girls with too much intensity. I think she knows.*

*She told me I belong to her. I laughed. She didn't.*

My fingers tremble as I turn the pages.

*Her rage is louder than her love, but her body still sings for me.*

*She said if I ever left her, she'd make sure no one else ever had me.*

"Roman," I say, softly.

The room drops in temperature. His presence floods in like mist.

"Tell us the rest."

Silence.

I brush my fingers over the soft page of the journal.

*I fear the day she realises I cannot return her in full—not what she wants. Not the way she wants it.*

*She sees the others. She sees my hands on them. My brush on their skin. My desire stretched too thin across too many faces. But Adeline wants to be my only masterpiece.*

My throat tightens.

"Roman," I whisper, louder now. "Tell us."

He doesn't answer in words at first.

Just a pressure. A pull.

Then—his voice, close, quiet, raw.

"She knew about the others," he says at last.

Nate shudders beside me and I take his hand, reassuring him.

"I thought she didn't care. In fact, for a long time she enjoyed our group as much as I did. She wanted to be loved, not just painted. I needed the beauty, the chaos, the devotion. I needed her... until I didn't."

He pauses. The shadows crawl deeper into the corners of the study.

"The night she died... she came to me in the bedroom in the dead of night stinking of whiskey and sex. But our company had left hours before. She asked if I would paint her one last time. I thought she meant it as a goodbye. A gift. But it wasn't. It was a trap."

"She killed you," I say.

"Yes."

Nate shifts beside me, arms crossed, his face drawn tight.

"She murdered you." Nate's voice is a command. A demand.

Roman doesn't answer immediately.

"She said if she couldn't have me in life, she'd have me in death. She opened my wrists on the bed where we fucked and fought and lived. Then she drove the letter opener into her own throat as I lay there, helpless to prevent it. She bled into the silk, then staggered to the window where she fell. I had to watch her die before my own life slipped away completely."

"She tethered you both here." My voice cracks, thick with emotion.

He doesn't respond. But the silence speaks for him.

The silence stretches long.

Roman lingers, his presence thick and aching. Nate squeezes my hand, but his eyes are locked on the painting across the room—Adeline, immortal and angry in oil.

"She tethered you both here," I say again, softer this time.

Finally, Roman speaks.

"Yes."

"But you're not bound to this house," Nate says. "Not in the same way she is."

"No. Not since you... opened me."

A shiver runs through me. I remember it now. That first night. The touch, the breath, the way I invited him in.

"I let you in," I murmur.

"You let me live."

"Then why can't we send her away without sending you too?" Nate asks.

"Because she is woven into the walls. Into the fabric of this place. Her death made her strong. Violent. Territorial. She will not go without a fight—and if we call her out, she will try to take everything with her."

"So what do we do?" My voice is firm, but burning for an

answer.

There's a pause.

Then Roman's voice brushes against my thoughts with a different weight. He sounds… cautious.

"You bind me."

I blink. "What?"

"To you, Dove. Voluntarily. Willingly. You let me anchor to your life—your soul—so I no longer depend on this house to remain. Once I'm bound to you, you can drive her out without banishing me too."

Nate goes very still beside me.

"That sounds like possession." His voice is low, cautious.

"No. Not like that. A tether, not a takeover. A thread of me, bound in love, in trust. Not in death."

"You want me to let you in deeper?" I whisper.

"It is the only way."

"It's a risk," Nate says. "A big one."

I nod. "I know."

Roman doesn't pressure. He just waits. His presence cool and quiet and full of longing.

I look down at the journal in my lap. The final entries stained with desperation. And I realise I'm not afraid of Roman. Not really. I'm afraid of what happens if I let him go.

# CHAPTER THIRTEEN

We spend the rest of the day preparing everything.

It has to be dark. That's how it always works. Spirit work is about invitation, about thresholds. And night opens the door.

We clear the dining room—push the chairs back, sweep the floor, wipe down the scarred old table until the surface gleams. Nate sets up cameras. We don't need to document this for anyone else. This is for us.

I draw the sigils from memory—chalk spirals and symbols etched into the wood. It's not the kind of magic you learn in books. It's older than that. The kind passed down in whispers, in touch, in gut instinct. I've only done this once before, and never like this.

Roman hovers nearby, silent and watchful. Nate lights the candles one by one until the room is bathed in soft gold and flickering shadow. No electric light. No cold logic. Just wax and fire and breath.

The chalk dust smudges across my bare forearms as I move around the table. The scratches from Adeline have faded now, but I still feel them when I glance at the skin. The mark she left wasn't just physical.

I wouldn't normally attempt a seance in a house this possessed. It's sheer idiocy. I know that in my rational brain. But I'm not being rational right now. I'm acting on emotion. I know it. Nate knows it. Roman definitely knows.

We bring in the cracked mirror from the landing, propping it against the wall that joins the dining room to the kitchen. The dull and tarnished surface reflects everything with a layer of distortion. But it's something Adeline has touched with her power. We couldn't possibly move that bed, so this will do.

I sit at the head of the table, and Nate sits around the corner of it to my left. We clasp hands, and each lay our other hand on the wooden surface, allowing space for Roman. He's as much a part of this as we are.

This is it. The mood is set. The candles flicker, and the soft scent of sulphur seeps under the door.

"This is where I speak for the dead," I murmur. "Where I become the gate."

Nate nods, solemn. He's here. With me. With us.

I close my eyes.

"Roman."

A hush falls, like the house itself is listening.

"I'm ready."

His presence wraps around me like fog, cold but welcome. Familiar. It slides over my skin like moonlight, settling across my shoulders, my chest, the nape of my neck. I feel his touch and his intention. He wants in.

Nate's hand tightens around mine.

"You're not alone," he murmurs.

A candle flickers violently to our right. The sulphur thickens in the air. Behind us, the mirror hums faintly—almost inaudible, but there.

"I open the gate," I say softly. "I welcome only one. Only

him."

A cold wind skims across the table. The flame closest to the mirror extinguishes. The air shimmers with tension.

The chalk sigils pulse faintly under my palms. Roman coils around my spine like smoke, waiting for my word. The candlelight paints Nate's face in gold and shadow—his eyes locked on mine, full of want and warning.

"Roman. I invite you in."

Roman breathes through me.

Nate slides his fingers to the nape of my neck, grounding me. I lean into him.

The candles flicker. One flares suddenly, bright and wild. I feel it in my chest—her. Not here, not fully. Just pressing. Watching. Jealous.

But not strong enough to break in. Not yet.

"She's close," I murmur. "We don't have much time."

Nate nods. His thumb traces the edge of my collarbone. I turn my head and press a kiss to his wrist. His pulse thuds strong against my lips.

Roman slips closer. His chill trails over the bare skin of my arms. Not threatening. Just claiming. His fingers glide down my ribcage, stopping just above the waistband of my jeans.

My breath catches.

Nate watches me, his hand still resting at my throat.

"Are you okay?" he asks.

"I don't know," I whisper. "But I want it."

"That's enough."

Our lips meet in a kiss ripe with urgency and longing. Every movement weighted with purpose. Nate's warmth spreads through me, one hand sliding beneath my shirt to cup my breast. Roman's touch follows, spectral and cool, coaxing my nipple to a tight peak. The contrast makes me shiver.

I press my thighs together, aching already. Roman hums in approval.

I pull out of the kiss and get shakily to my feet.

"She's close," I whisper. "But she hasn't pushed through."

"Then let's keep going," Nate murmurs.

I nod. I slip off my shirt. Nate rises just enough to unbutton my jeans, his fingers brushing my skin.

Roman kisses my shoulder—not lips, not flesh, but a brush of cold so intimate it steals my breath.

"You feel so much," he whispers aloud now. "Even when you're afraid."

"Especially when I'm afraid," I reply with a light laugh.

Nate chuckles under his breath. "That explains a lot."

I lie back on the table. Naked from the waist up. The chalk dust streaks across my skin. My jeans hang open. Roman's fingers trail down my hips, and Nate leans in to kiss the hollow of my throat.

It builds. Touch by touch. Kiss by kiss.

And then—

A gust of wind slams against the window.

The mirror creaks.

The temperature drops.

The candle nearest the mirror flares and explodes—wax spraying the edge of the table.

I flinch.

Roman recoils.

Nate catches my arm. "Hey. You're okay."

I push up to sitting, heart pounding.

"She's pushing. She knows."

"She's not strong enough."

"She will be."

Nate rests his forehead to mine. "So what do you want to

do?"

I look at the ruined candle. The mirror.

Then at the sigils glowing faintly beneath me.

"She can't stop this," I say. "Not if we keep going."

Roman's voice murmurs beside my ear. "You have to let me all the way in."

A chill rolls through me. Not from fear. From memory. And suddenly, I'm not just here. I'm seventeen again. A stranger's attic. A stupid dare. Four girls, two candles, one cracked Ouija board.

The plan was to ask if the house was haunted. A little urban-legend thrill. The others laughed when I said I'd go under, let someone speak through me. I thought I was bluffing too. Until I wasn't.

He came through the moment I touched the board.

Not Roman. Something else. Older. Colder. Wrong.

He whispered through me. Took my voice. My breath. He said my name. Not the one I gave. The one no one else knew.

It took six hours to shake him loose.

No one believed what I remembered. They just said I passed out. Had a seizure. But I knew. He tried to stay. Tried to make me his. And I never told anyone how close I came to letting him.

Because part of me liked it.

"I've done this before," I whisper.

Nate looks at me. "What?"

I shake my head. "Another time. Another spirit. Not a ghost. Not like Roman. It almost destroyed me."

Roman is still, a cold, steady presence in the room. "I know," he says. "I felt the wound when I entered you."

"Then you know why I need to be sure."

"I won't take what isn't given."

Another candle goes out.

The mirror groans.

I scan the room and I see him, Roman, standing beside the table, one arm around Nate's shoulders, the other pressed to the runes nearest him on the table. He's beautiful. Young, lithe, alive.

"Do you promise, Roman? Do you swear that you mean no harm?"

"I do, my Dove. I have only love for you." He smiles and it lights up his whole face. Nate glances in his direction.

"Can you see him?" he whispers.

I nod.

"Say the words, Dove," Roman whispers. "Call me."

"I, Rae Holloway, call you, Roman, to dwell in me—not as master, not as shadow, but as bond. I open myself to you in trust, in truth, in blood and breath and body."

The chalk begins to glow.

Roman groans—a sound like longing unravelled. He rushes into me and swells inside my chest, my spine, my thighs.

Nate approaches, eyes locked on mine. "We're in this together." He tugs my jeans off and tosses them aside.

I watch as he unfastens his own.

Roman purrs inside me. Cold and hot all at once.

Nate's hands grasp my hips, and Roman's arms wrap around my body. Cold. Hot. Opposing. Entwined. In me. Around me.

"Are you sure?" Nate asks, searching my face.

"Yes," I whisper. "Both of you. Now."

I lie back.

The wood is hard beneath me, but I don't care. Nate climbs onto the table and covers me with his warm body. His mouth finds mine, hungry and searching.

Roman's breath coats my skin like mist. Their touches

blend—one warm and grounding, the other chilled and electric. I'm a bridge. A body of fire and frost.

Nate enters me with a slow, deep thrust.

Roman slides into my mind, into my soul, with equal pressure.

I cry out—pure, honest sound—and the candles flare white.

I feel everything.

Above us, the ceiling shakes and the light fitting swings angrily from side to side, like a hypnotist's pocket watch. My gaze follows it for a moment, but I close my eyes and anchor myself on the table.

Nate thrusts hard and fast, filling me, stretching me in the best way.

Roman moves out of me and surrounds Nate. Wrapping himself around Nate's body. The two men merge and Nate's head flies back. His eyes glow softly white and a harsh gasp shudders from his parted lips.

"Oh God!"

The silvery light of Roman slithers out of Nate and passes back into me. My body is fire and ice all at once as I come. My body convulses on the table. My knees grip Nate's hips, my nails dig into his shoulders.

"Yes!" I cry out, my voice echoing back to me.

Adeline screams. Her horror splits the ceiling and dust rains down on Nate's back.

But he keeps going, pounding hard into me. Throbbing. Moaning.

Roman's climax ripples through me like an invocation. Icy cold and burning hot. He sears himself into my soul.

Nate groans above me, clutching my hands tight and pressing them hard into the table. His hips jerk as he comes, releasing into me with wild abandon.

The symbols on the table blaze, briefly, and then burn out, seared into the wood.

"I'm yours now," Roman breathes aloud. "Bound. Blood and breath and body."

My vision blurs. Nate collapses onto my chest, breathless. Roman's presence pulses in my veins.

Outside, the wind howls.

And upstairs, Adeline screams.

# CHAPTER FOURTEEN

The scream doesn't stop.

It claws down the walls, rattles the windows, shudders through the bones of the house like a quake of rage.

I scramble upright, legs shaky, my skin slick with sweat and sex and chalk dust. Nate rolls off the table with a groan, catching himself on the edge before his ankle buckles.

Candles extinguish one by one—snuffed out by a wind that doesn't exist.

The mirror in the corner vibrates in its frame, the cracked glass warping our reflections into things neither of us recognise.

"She knows she's losing him," I breathe, steadying myself.

"She's not going easy," Nate growls. His voice is ragged, throat raw from the scream of climax—and now, from fear.

Roman's voice curls through my chest.

"She can't touch me now. But she can still touch you."

A gust of cold slams into the room.

Nate is knocked back against the wall, the air ripped from his lungs.

"Nate!" I shout, reaching for him—too late. He crumples to the floor, gasping, one hand clutching his ribs.

A shadow pools in the mirror.

It peels away from the glass.

Adeline.

Not the bleeding woman from the dream. Not the painting. Not even the glamour from Roman's memory. This is her—unveiled, unbound, and furious.

Her eyes are black pits. Her mouth stretches impossibly wide. Her fingers drip with something too dark to be blood. The smell of iron and rot fills the air.

"You took him from me."

Her voice splits through my skull. Not sound. Intent.

I brace myself against the table. The runes are dark, burned into the wood. The sex magic lives here. Roman lives in me now.

I scream back.

"He was never yours!"

Adeline flies at me.

A blur of shadows and shrieking light. Her scream is in my teeth, in my spine, in my womb. She doesn't want to scare me—she wants to crack me open.

Roman surges up inside me, cold and brilliant. "Stand your ground," he commands. "She can't pass the circle unless you let her."

I slam my hand to the table—our sigils, still seared into the wood, flare to life under my touch, bright and hot. The blast of light forces Adeline back, howling.

Nate drags himself upright, hand braced on a chair. "What do we do?"

I answer without hesitation. "We finish it."

I leap down from the table, naked, furious, alive. The fear doesn't go—but it burns in my chest like fuel.

Adeline flickers—three places at once, like a glitch in reality. Her body is beginning to break apart. She's losing her anchor.

Losing her grip.

She screams again.

"You took him. You broke the chain. I bled for him!"

"And now you'll let him go," I say. "This house is no longer yours."

She lunges. Her mouth opens wider than it should, splitting her jaw like a snake unhinging.

"You took him," she hisses through cracked glass and cracked time. "You used his body like a whore."

My hands curl into fists. Roman coils behind my ribs like a blade drawn clean.

"He chose me," I shout. "You never owned him."

"Liar."

And I feel it—the moment she pushes through.

My shield shatters.

The cold rushes into me like drowning.

I scream.

Nate stumbles forward—but Adeline is faster. Her hands seize my throat, and suddenly I'm inside the memory of her death—the bedroom, the blood, her smile as she died. It's fast. A blur really and I struggle to hold onto it, like trying to grasp smoke. Was that her bloody hand on the letter opener? Or someone else's?

With a jolt, I'm back in the dining room.

"I died for him," she snarls. "I gave everything."

The air leaves my lungs. Roman's voice frays in my head.

Rae— I'm losing you—don't let go—

My body jerks.

Nate grabs Adeline from behind, arms locking through hers—but it's like grabbing wind and fire and grief. She screams and throws him across the room—he slams into the wall with a sickening crunch and collapses.

"Nate!" My voice rips from me as I fall to my knees beside him. His eyes flutter. There's blood in his mouth.

Adeline looms behind me. "One last thing, before I take you with me."

Her hand plunges toward my chest.

And I remember the attic.

That first time.

The whisper of something dark and ancient, trying to wear me like a coat.

But now I know the difference.

Now I'm not alone.

Roman rises like a storm inside me.

"No," I gasp. "Not again."

I shove up from the floor, hands blazing with chalk-light. Adeline shrieks—but this time it sounds more human. Like heartbreak.

"By my body," I say. "By my blood."

Candles explode outward—Roman's power surging through me.

"By the bond I claimed and the love you tried to bury—I cast you out!"

A rift opens in the air. Light tears through the walls. Adeline is yanked backward, clawing at the floor, sobbing now—screams fading into silence.

And then—

Gone.

Silence settles like dust.

No scream. No wind. No flickering light.

Just the echo of what we did, hanging in the charged stillness of the room.

I don't move right away. I can't. My hands are trembling, my breath stuttering. My knees are still pressed to the floorboards, hot with the echo of magic.

Across from me, Nate groans.

I crawl to him, my limbs clumsy with adrenaline and exhaustion.

"Nate," I whisper, brushing hair from his forehead. He blinks up at me, one eye already swelling. Blood paints the corner of his mouth. His ribs rise unevenly beneath my hand.

"Still alive?" he rasps.

"Barely."

He laughs—then winces. "Let's not do that again."

I press my forehead to his. "Agreed."

Roman moves inside me like a ripple. No longer a storm. No longer frantic. Just present.

"I'm here," he murmurs. "You did it."

"We did it," I whisper.

The house is still.

No creaking. No whispering.

Even the oppressive chill is gone.

"What time is it?" Nate mumbles.

I glance toward the nearest camera—its tiny red light still blinking, miraculously untouched.

"Late," I say. "Or early."

"I think I dislocated something."

"Yeah," I murmur, brushing my fingers along his bruised side. "You should probably lie still."

Nate blinks again, slower this time. "Was it worth it?"

I don't answer right away. I look around the room—at the shattered mirror, the extinguished candles, the sigils scorched into the table.

At the silence.

At the space where Adeline was.

And the warmth inside me now where Roman is.

"Yes," I say softly. "It was worth it."

I get Nate to the sofa with Roman's help—or rather, my strength bolstered by Roman's silent guidance. Nate hisses as he eases down, clutching his ribs. I cover him with the blanket, retrieve a bottle of water, clean the worst of the blood from his mouth. He's bruised. Battered. But very much alive.

We don't talk.

We just rest.

Eventually, I lie down beside him, curling into the curve of his body. He pulls me close with the arm that still works, his other arm limp against his side. I press a kiss to the hollow beneath his throat.

"I'm so fucking glad you're not dead," I murmur.

"Me too," he replies. "I'd really hate to miss what comes next."

We drift like that—wrapped in silence and sweat and blankets.

And somewhere in the spaces between, Roman curls around us both.

His voice low and warm in my mind.

"I won't leave. Not unless you ask me to."

Sunlight streams through the windows. Real light. Clean. No shadows on the ceiling. No distorted faces in the glass. Just light.

Nate groans as he tries to sit up. "Every bone I have is staging a coup."

I help him move slowly, rewrapping his ribs and ankle with fresh tape. He winces, but lets me.

The house is quiet.

Peaceful.

And I realise—we've never heard it like this before. No creaks. No whispers. No breath behind breath. It's a house again. Just a house.

We dress and pack slowly. Carefully.

Nate packs the damaged cameras in their padded cases. I fold up the cables. Neither of us wants to say what we're both thinking. Roman is quiet, but I feel him watching.

When I start coiling the final cord, I pause. I turn to Nate.

"I don't want to leave."

He looks up at me. "Yeah. Me neither."

Roman stirs.

"You don't have to."

I glance toward the staircase, where the worst things happened. And still... I feel drawn to stay. Like the house has been remade, rewired by everything we did here.

Roman's voice grows brighter. "So many memories. Good ones. You remade this place. You filled it with love."

Nate meets my eyes. "It would make a hell of a headquarters."

I smile. "We'd have to buy it."

Roman hums. "I'll behave. I promise."

I arch an eyebrow. "Define 'behave'."

But he doesn't answer—he just wraps around my spine again like a silken thread, like a sigh.

Nate stands, wobbly but upright, and limps toward me.

I meet him halfway.

We hold each other for a long time, and I feel him. And I feel Roman. And something else entirely that only the three of us make together.

Outside, the wind moves through the trees.

And the house—for the first time—feels like it's breathing with us, not against us.

Nate pulls back slightly and brushes a strand of hair from my cheek. "So what now?"

I smile.

"We go home."

He lifts a brow. "Where's that, exactly?"

I glance around the room.

"This," I say. "Feels like a good start."

And inside me, Roman whispers, tender and certain—

"Ours."

# The Bookbinder's Farewell

*Still here?*

I thought you might be.

Some stories don't end. They echo. They haunt.

You followed Rae into the dark. You let Roman inside. You saw what happens when grief turns to devotion and devotion turns to something *far more dangerous*.

Now you understand.

Some hauntings aren't curses. They're invitations.

And darling, this is only the beginning.

My next stories are louder. Filthier. More demanding.

I've been gentle long enough.

*Come back when you're ready to be ruined properly.*

# The Heat Doesn't Have to End Here

*Want more of this possessive threesome?*

Sign up to my newsletter for exclusive bonus content—including epilogues you won't find anywhere else.
It's free, filthy, and just a little bit forbidden.

Download it here: https://BookHip.com/RSJCBZG

See you between the pages, gorgeous.
Lacey xox

Printed in Dunstable, United Kingdom

67768201R00071